I0518275

Grimm and Grimmer
Volume Four

Edited By

Colin Fisher

EDITED BY COLIN FISHER

COVER BY PAPER PANDA LTD

Introduction © Sarah Pinborough

The Robber Bride © Sara Taylor

The Bear's Coat © David Moore

Grisel and Fairy Obvious © Julius Horne

The Mouse, the Bird and the Sausage © Kirstin Fulton

Once Upon a Time © Leland Thoburn

The Frag Prince © Andrew Lawston

The Debt We Must All Pay © L F Robertson

Afterword © Colin Fisher

Cover Design and Artwork © Paper Panda Ltd

Copyright © 2016 Fringeworks Ltd

ISBN: 978-1-909573-27-7

Published 2016

Fringeworks Ltd, Y Berllan, Maen Y Groes, Cei Newydd,
Ceredigion, SA45 9TR.

The right of the authors to be identified as the authors
of this work has been asserted in accordance with the
Copyright, Designs and Patents Act 1988. All rights
reserved. No part of this publication may be reproduced,
stored in a retrieval system, or transmitted, in any form
or by any means, electronic, mechanical, photocopying,
recording or otherwise, without the prior permission of
the copyright owners.

CONTENTS

INTRODUCTION
by Sarah Pinborough

There are few more comforting words in the English language than 'Once upon a time', words that have the ability to so quickly transport us back to a time in our lives when fiction and reality were intertwined and nothing seemed impossible. Princes, witches, dwarfs, trolls, princesses, magic, and happily ever afters sprang into our childhood minds just with that one opening phrase.

It's no wonder, then, that Fairy Tales are never far from our western cultural consciousness. From their dark and violent origins they grew into the slightly less aggressive versions that the Grimm brothers collected, and then morphed into Disneyfied saccharine gloriously coloured animated movies beloved around the world. More recently, they have had another cinematic revival with films such as Snow White and the Huntsman, and on TV 'Once upon a Time' gave the characters we know and love a new life in its own engaging take on the world of Fairy Tales.

Within literature both Neil Gaiman and Philip Pullman are amongst those who have turned their hand to re-tellings, and, as it should be with stories that started in the oral tradition, each time these works are re-presented, something at their core shifts and they are changed, each new version adding a new layer to the familiar tropes. As the world around us changes, what we want from fairy tales changes too. Not every girl wants to grow up to marry a Prince Charming and live in a castle and push out babies. Not all beauty is good and all ugliness, wicked. True love does not always conquer all. Our world is complex and our lives complicated, and the morals and messages we need come down to more than just assigned gender roles.

In Grimm & Grimmer 4, there are seven fairy tales, retold, to delight you and add their own textures to those stories of old. Some you will recognise quickly, others have taken various elements of various fairy tales and woven them into something new, but I promise you humour, darkness, imagination, politics, religion, a good comeuppance, and of course, love. There is the first world and a land so far, far away it's definitely alien. You will smile, and you will think and I can't think of a better purpose for any story than to make you smile and make you think.

I can't promise you a happy ever after for all of these stories, but I can promise you a happy afternoon reading them.

Are you sitting comfortably?

Then let us begin.

THE ROBBER BRIDE

by Sara Taylor

I

I hoped that when I met Sir Michael Frobisher, my betrothed, I would feel the sort of spark, the lightning through the gut the girls in my dancing class described as love. Or else utter revulsion. I hoped to feel something; I wasn't too particular about what it was. He was a tall man, dark haired and blue eyed, well-proportioned and decked out in silks that were expensive but not extravagant. Though I knew that I should be swooning over his looks, if not his purse, I could not find it in myself. He could have been a bundle of firewood, he moved me so little.

He did speak prettily to me on that meeting, called me beautiful and clever, and presented me with a betrothal ring to mark the occasion. I smiled as best I could - it was a gaudy thing, with a ruby the size of a robin's egg - and so he teased me with a story about it, that it was a magic ring that would lead me to his house were I ever in distress. I didn't know what to say to that, so I said nothing.

I put him quite out of my mind for the next few days, but I could not ignore the weight of that ring. It was heavy on my hand, the band around my finger itched, but when I took it off the housekeeper chided me so sharply that I put it immediately on again. The girls at dancing class remarked on it admiringly, asked me to describe him, and since it got me their full attention I didn't mind it so much.

Some nights later I woke in the darkness with the most powerful compulsion to go outside. Thinking I just needed air, I dressed and went down into the courtyard, but once there the compulsion grew stronger, and almost against my will I undid the latch and passed through the garden gate and into the lamp-shadowed streets, around bends and turns as crooked as a dog's back legs, through the little man-sized gate besides the cart-sized gate in the city walls, and into the surrounding forest.

I had never been beyond the walls alone. The darkness did not frighten me; fairy tales had not been encouraged in my nursery and so my world was not peopled with talking wolves and malevolent sprites, but by sleeping birds and beasts. A broad path opened up before me, and I followed its twists to a little thatched house, half-timbered and neat as a pin. I was dreaming, I thought, and so I went in.

The first room was furnished with a broad table, surrounded by high-backed hearth benches draped with heavily furred hides, the sitting room of someone whose tastes ran more to hunting than to dancing. A small, piping voice came to me, the sound of someone singing the sort of folk tune that doubles back and repeats itself, and I followed the sound into the room beyond.

The great table in the centre of the room was cleared, though stained and scarred, but the sideboards were crammed with covered dishes and pans, and the corners crowded with casks and barrels. The singer, a tiny woman perched on a stool at the hearth with her back to me, prodded the kettle with a blackened poker. This being a dream, or so I thought, I expected her to be a wizened crone of the sort that would dispense hard-won wisdom in rhyme, but when she heard my step in the doorway and turned to face me I was surprised to see that she was no older than I. Her face was narrow and sharp and birdlike, and when she hopped down from the stool and shuffled over to me her movements were birdlike as well, hampered by a heavy manacle and length of chain that attached her ankle to a ring in the stonework of the fireplace.

"May I help you, miss?" she asked, and I felt my heart beat faster.

I'd spent time with girls my age before, but though I found them pleasant to watch and listen too, I had never before felt the rising in my belly that I did when Muireen first spoke, like cider poured too fast so that it foams over the lip of the vessel. She was freckled all over like the speckling of a plover's egg, dirty, underfed: the most perfect woman I had ever seen.

"I... I don't rightly know," I said.

"Would you like to sit down then, and have a think on it?" she asked, and pulled out one of the chairs so that I could sit at the table. "The tea water is nearly boiling, and I'm certain I have tarts about somewhere. You've come alone?" I watched her as she scurried about making the tea and plating some cakes, the chain rattling after her, cheeks flushing slowly with embarrassment at my staring.

"It's the oddest thing," I said as she swished the tealeaves in a yellow pot. "I woke from sleep and walked as though fate led me. There was no path save for the one to this house." I looked her in her eyes - so deep a blue they appeared nearly black at a distance - and she flushed deeper, then noted the ring on my hand.

"And this would be why," she said, and touched it lightly, as though it burned her. "There's a magic to this house that's quite beyond understanding. You'd better get yourself gone, miss, before the master gets back."

"How long have you been here?" I asked, quite determined to stay as long as it took to win her confidence. Her master would hardly cast me out of the house in the middle of the night, and as I was doing nothing more than sitting in the warmth I couldn't imagine him even being very angry with her or me.

"Since I was seven years old," she answered. "He brought me here on horseback from the market on the docks, and a blacksmith fixed the chain about my ankle the same day. I've not stirred from this room since." She paced back and refilled the kettle, then resumed her perch on the stool by the hearth, the chain dangling and clinking from beneath the hem of her tattered petticoat.

"Have you found it lonely?"

"Loneliness is better than the alternative," she shuddered. "The master has been my only company, and life is altogether more pleasant when he is away from the house, miss."

"What does he do to make you prefer the silence?" I dropped my voice as I asked, but her look became immediately guarded.

"I wouldn't wish to turn your stomach with lurid tales, miss. He'll be returning, and you'll want to be far gone from this place before he does."

"But I find your company quite pleasant," I said, and sipped at the tea she had given me. "And so many years alone, it would be cruel to leave you to your empty kitchen when I have so recently arrived."

She repeated her caution, then turned to coaxing, and then begging, but I found myself determined to remain. She finally surrendered to my will, and sat next to me at the table and told me what she remembered of her life before coming to the enchanted house, and of her days in it. At first she was hesitant, but as she spoke her voice became more fluid, as though a dam inside her were slowly crumbling away to let the words flow freely, and as I watched her face become more animated and her eyes glow more hotly the fizzing in my belly rose to a dull ache in my chest. I wanted to touch her, to push back the cloth that covered her hair so I could run my fingers through it, to kiss each and every freckle. I wondered what she would think if I did so, or what she would do. Perhaps she would have welcomed it, but I didn't know how best to ask, or what words to use, so nebulous and strange was my longing.

As she rose to boil another kettle there came a thump at the outer door, and we both jumped as though stuck with a thousand needles. My bravado of earlier waned at the prospect of actually meeting her master, but Muireen positively blanched in terror. There was a second thump, and the sound of raucous singing, and she sprang to me and dragged me up by an arm and thrust me behind the barrels in a corner, her stricken face conveying clearer than words that I was to make no sound nor movement.

No sooner was I huddled tight among the barrels then a clutch of men trooped in: three in all, with my betrothed leading the way. Muireen dropped to her knees before them, head bowed, and he aimed a box at her ear and bellowed for her to fetch drink. There were also two women, already half drunk and their clothing half off, billing and cooing and stealing kisses from the men and each other. The men sat where I had not moments before and pulled the women onto their laps, downed great mugs of foaming beer and exchanged lewd stories, their laughter growing more and more boisterous. Then, as though he could not wait any longer, my betrothed hefted one of the women onto the table and climbed up afterwards.

I had never thought I would witness what they then proceeded to do, while the three remaining cheered them on and continued to drink, though the kitchen girls had described it to me quite inaccurately and with many giggles. The sight simultaneously intrigued and horrified me, so that I found myself unable to take my eye away from the gap between the barrels through which I watched the whole affair. Muireen had retreated to the farthest corner, and the others were deep in their cups, so I was the only one to see his hands creeping closer and closer to her throat, and to realize what he was after as he began to squeeze and her face to color. She struggled against him and cried out hoarsely for some minutes and then was still, while the others redoubled their noise. I thought they had taken her panic for enjoyment, but when the second woman realized her companion was dead she started up a screaming, and the two men took her up to hush her in the same way my betrothed had hushed his, permanently. I could not look any more, and hid my eyes in my arms, struggling to keep from being sick.

There was silence then, except for their laughter.

"Girl, fetch me a cleaver! This one's fingers have grown so fat that I'll have to cut them off to get at her rings."

I heard the rattle of Muireen's chain, and then the sickening thud of a blade biting the table. They continued their chat, and the thud of the blade sounded again, and I rocked in place behind the barrels. The next thud was twinned by a muffled thump as something tiny alighted in my lap, in the folds of skirts between my knees, and I took it up before I realized what it was: a human finger, the long nail rough at the edge, still adorned with a scratched and tarnished silver ring. As the scream rose within me, Muireen caught my eye through the crack, and the fear on her face stifled me in time.

"Where has it gone?" one of the men cried out, and fell to looking in the cracks between the flagstones.

"Don't tell me you've lost it," my betrothed thundered back to him. "Girl, a filleting knife! We've not the patience to let these two conies hang." He began butchering the first of the two girls with deft strokes while Muireen scurried about fetching water and knives and rags and setting cuts to roast or boil as he ordered. The second man continued to drink, watching the strokes of my bridegroom's knife with glassy eyes, but the third continued to hunt about in the dust for the lost finger, until I grew certain that he would find me.

"Leave it be for now, Will," my betrothed hollered at him as the man blundered into his ankles. "It won't get up and walk off between now and morning, and it was only a silver ring. Come and enjoy your dinner, man!"

I felt as though I would die of old age, or sooner of horror, as I watched them butcher the women and set to drinking as Muireen mopped the blood from the table and served them thick slabs of roasted flesh. She could have been made of wood for all the notice they paid her, but as they grew sated one of them pulled her onto his lap and thrust a hand into her bodice.

"The only issue with this manner of doing things is that it leaves no means of satisfaction afterwards, hey Michael?" He tried to steal a kiss as she struggled.

"Let my help be; she's for scrubbing floors, not warming beds," he answered. "If you're so frantic for satisfaction we can find another pair of whores."

He reluctantly unhanded her and she scurried once again as far from them as her chain would allow.

"'Tis a pity," the man belched. "Tethered birds are the most sport to shoot, and have the sweetest meat and the loudest cry when finally caught."

Her master called, and Muireen came reluctantly to clear the table, staying as far out of reach as possible, though it did not save her completely from slaps and pinches. It lit a burning in me to see them treat her so, though at the same time I wondered guiltily what it would feel like to pull her onto my lap in the same manner.

As the front door slammed shut behind them Muireen came to my hiding place.

"Please, miss, get you gone before they come back. I don't want to see you killed and that's surely what they'll do if they find you here, and most like me as well."

I wanted to kiss her, to hold her, to tell her that I would take her away from this place. Instead, my mouth gaped like a fish's for a moment, so full of words that none would come out, and she thrust me through the door.

The woods were dark and silent still, as though I had spent no more than a minute in the house, though surely it had been half the night, and I ran straight and true as an arrow through the trees until the light of town and home rose out of the darkness to guide me. No one noted my passage through the gates, through the garden, and into my own quiet room.

When I woke the next morning I thought I had been dreaming; I had had strange and vivid dreams of beautiful women before, though I did not like to own it even to myself. But as I finished my breakfast and went to fill my pocket with walnuts from the sideboard as I was in the habit of doing, I found something soft and cold already there. Dread rose in me, and I went back to my room before drawing the object out, even though I knew what it would be: a severed finger, blue and bloodless, adorned with a tarnished silver ring.

II

The weeks passed leadenly. I cast about the house for a means of rescuing Muireen, but found that my comfortable home was not well outfitted with the tools necessary to free a prisoner. Finally, I bribed one of the stable boys to find me a set of skeleton keys, the type that will open any lock, and slept with it strung about my neck on a ribbon, in case I woke again and was drawn to the house. That this would happen I was certain, as every time I had set out on my own to find it I had not felt the pull of the ring nor been able to even leave the house.

Of my betrothal I perhaps thought not enough. I felt that somehow it would not come, that if I rescued Muireen we would together make a life for ourselves elsewhere, though I had no more idea how we would as how I might sprout wings and fly.

When the ring drew me I was ready for it, and fairly ran down the wooded paths and up to the cottage door. The pull came earlier than I had expected, at twilight, and though I half-wondered if Sir Frobisher was home I pushed through the door anyway, trusting that the ring would not have led me there for me to be cut down and eaten.

Muireen was chopping marrows with her back to me when I entered, silent this time. She jumped and turned when I called her name, blushed scarlet, looked away, whispered, "I wanted you to come back."

I didn't know what to say, couldn't stop myself from running my fingertips across her freckled cheek, then into the thick, soft hair at the back of her neck, then finally from pulling her close to me and pressing my mouth to hers. Her lips were sweet and soft and cool, and opened to mine like the petals of the first spring flowers.

For long minutes we stood, sharing each other's breath and life, and it was so much easier than I had imagined it would be when I'd lain awake through the long nights waiting for the ring to draw me to her. When we finally stepped apart her face was bright scarlet, but with excitement rather than shame or anger, and it was all I could do to not take her up again and continue where we'd left off.

She reached to my neckline, and my heart beat hard, but all she did was fish out the bunch of skeleton keys from their place between my breasts.

"So that's what was digging into me," she grinned, and reached down a small bottle of cooking oil from the shelf.

We worked the keys in one by one, coated the works of the lock and our hands and her ankle with the oil, jiggled and pressed and played with it for long minutes before we both had to admit that the lock had rusted shut. It was as stiff as if there had been no lock at all, just a solid metal bracelet about her ankle, the skin beneath it scarred and bruised. She looked up at me as we sat there, tears in her eyes but her chin firm.

"You'll think of something," she said.

I pulled her down onto the floor with me and lay there with her in my arms for long minutes, kissing away our tears and disappointments. It was with reluctance that I finally let her coax me up and to the door.

As the days passed I turned my mind to other ways that I might free her, though through the nights I confess my thoughts were not so pure. The solution came to me, quite by accident, at the hands of my betrothed. He had taken to visiting quite regularly, as if I were a wild creature that he could acclimate to his presence, and on one of these visits he chanced to mention that I would need a handmaid when I came to his house.

"I suppose if I cannot take a woman from my father's house, then I would like a young girl, so as to have a clean slate to inscribe with my particular needs and fancies," I said when he first brought it up, and he promised to find me a girl young and fresh before our wedding day.

"Have you ever seen a girl with red hair?" I then asked him. He said that he had, once. "I don't suppose such people are born very often?" He admitted that they weren't, but if I were determined to have an oddity as a maid, then I would have it, if he had to scour the earth to find such a woman. As he left me I crossed my fingers in hope.

The day before our wedding the housekeeper called me down to the kitchen where he had brought Muireen, washed and neatly dressed, her chain cut, for my inspection. She kept her eyes on the ground, but still it was all I could do to remain calm, to run her hair through my fingers as though I were stroking a mare's tale, to trace my hands over her freckled skin and then finally declare her perfect in every way.

III

As the guests congregated in the atrium of my father's house the housekeeper and her minions decked me in my wedding finery, but when they left me I slipped out and down the hall to my father's private study.

I found him as I expected to, drinking with the Lord of the town and one or two important men I did not recognize. My father was surprised to see me, but I sank to my knees next to his seat before he could say anything.

They looked quite disbelieving as I told my tale, but when I drew out the finger, gone quite soft and lurid, though I had kept it in the ice cellar, all the men started up at once. The Lord's voice rose above all their cries of shock, and he called for the arrest of Sir Frobisher. My joy turned to horror as he called also for the arrest of all the servants of his household, for their complicity in the crime, and I was taken up and back to my chamber before I could make sense of it all.

As daylight faded I took off my frothing white, and then my jewels, but when I opened their casket I found again the string of skeleton keys I had thought to use to steal Muireen away.

No one noted my exit, pockets bulging with my dead mother's jewels. The first prison guard was bribed with a kiss, the second with a pearl earring. I told him that I had come to visit my sister, but after the pearl little begging was required before he allowed me to wander.

I let myself into her cell quietly, but she sprang upright at the jingle of the keys. We did not speak; she scurried out the moment I opened the door, and I tucked her under the spreading skirts of my gown and wandered slowly back out.

A street away, with Muireen still clinging to my legs, I felt the tug of the ring. We ran for the gate to the city, feet barely touching the ground. No one challenged us, and the forest opened up before us in a clear, broad path. As we drew near to the house I slowed, worried that somehow my bridegroom had also escaped the prison, but Muireen pulled me forward.

"We were to be executed at sunrise," she said as she pushed open the door. "He'll not be coming again, nor will any other man be able to find us."

She closed the door behind us, and I realized what we had done. What I had done. I stood then in my own house, pockets stuffed with jewels, quite beyond the reach of mortal man, with my sweetheart by my side. I drew her in to kiss her, but she brushed me away with a smile.

"There are bedrooms above stairs for that," she said. "You were supposed to consummate your marriage on this night; I think that's best done the proper way, as it's only done once."

She took me by the hand and led me gently up the stairs, to the bridal chamber.

THE BEAR'S COAT

by David Thomas Moore

The rifle's report is still ringing in his ears.

There's fear, of course, but muted, dulled. To some extent, he's relieved. He's spent years in fear, dreading death and hating himself for it; now it's happening, and he wonders, idly, why it loomed so large. It's not such a hard thing to do, in the end.

To some extent, he is incredulous. Now he dies?

His world is full of heat, of light. Of pain.

He remembers.

***

April, 1919. The century was not yet twenty years in, and already the world had seen the worst war in human reckoning. To the old soldier nursing a gin in the front bar, at the Old Bell in Hackney, it may as well have never ended.

He'd been home two years. Copped a Blighty One in the trenches and was sent to his eldest brother's to recover. An ugly scar marred his left shin, although he could walk now, barely ever needed the stick. It ached in the cold.

There was a pension. And there'd been work, of course. Hell, there were women in the factories still; a young man, even one crippled like himself, could take his pick of jobs.

He could never seem to stick at it, though. He lost his temper, started fights. Ended them. Two men with broken bones, so far, and a third spent a month in the hospital. His name got around, and it started to get harder to find new jobs. His brothers tried to help – one was a foreman at a car factory, the other a clerk in the City – but he failed there, too. Eventually, sympathy in their eyes, they had given up on him. Everyone had.

His old mates from the war had gone over the top six months after he'd left, and been killed to a man with half the battalion. Just him, left behind by chance.

Hardly ever had to buy his own drink, of course, not with a demob suit and a limp. There were plenty of girls, too. And he had his pension, and his brothers gave him a little money. But getting by wasn't enough for any man. You had to have something to do.

So this was where he'd wound up. Waiting to meet Sailor Jim, who was going to line him up with some other chaps, sort out some work. It wasn't lawful, wouldn't have made his dad all that proud, but it was something he could do.

He finished his gin, poured another, waited.

***

He remembers.

***

December, 1919. He and Tommy and Ernie were in the back room of the Rose and Crown, having a bit of a discussion with Sailor Jim. Jim wasn't convinced about his cut of the post office job. Reckoned they were too messy, attracted too much attention. Shouldn't have killed the cashier. The police were going to be looking for the money; Jim was going to be taking a bigger risk, and that risk should be rewarded appropriately.

They weren't having any of it. It was all getting a bit heated.

He went to grab Jim by the lapels of his coat, to give him a shake and press his point home, and Jim's enforcer stepped in.

Man was called "The Bear." He was a brute: six-foot-seven and twenty-five stone if he was an ounce. They said he ripped both a man's arms off once, at the same time. Just grabbed him by the elbows and off they'd both come, like breaking a wishbone. He doubted it was true, but you could just about believe it, to look at the man.

The Bear reached for him, grabbed his shoulder, and he acted before thinking, sinking his left fist into the giant's gut – felt like hitting wood – and lashing out for his throat with a right hook.

Most people looked at the limp, assumed he was a soft touch, but he was tough before the war, and a monster after. He was fast and strong, but it was more than that: he'd lose himself, forget about everything, fight like his life depended on it.

It was over quickly. He found himself standing over the Bear's body, blood on his hands, on his face.

Jim was staring at him, eyes as big as pennies. He was taken aback himself, wasn't sure how to react. Eventually, figuring it was better to brazen it out and deal with what he'd done later, he'd calmly wiped his hands off on his shirt, bent down and set about pulling off the Bear's coat.

The Bear had had this huge coat, a great furry thing you could wear in a Russian winter. It was as much the source of his nickname as his size and strength were.

It took a minute or so, heaving the massive enforcer's body around to heave it off – in truth, a little too long, dulling the impact of the gesture a little – but he eventually got it free and shrugged it on with a grim smile. Jim found his tongue again, and began quietly negotiating a fairer cut with Ernie.

That was when a lad he didn't know came down from upstairs and said the Gentleman wanted a word with him.

***

He remembers.

***

Everyone knew about the Gentleman. Jim was the don at the Rose and Crown, and about half a dozen other places around the area; he had at least a dozen little outfits like Ernie's on his books. But the Gentleman was Jim's don, and had a few other dons under his umbrella besides; if you believed the talk, he ran most of the thieves and killers in London. There was other talk about him, weird talk, but... well.

People talk, don't they?

He wore a black velvet three-piece over a smart silk shirt. His hair was blond and wavy, and he affected a small moustache; his eyes were the colour of ice, and his smile never reached them. He moved stiffly, sometimes, as though an old back wound troubled him.

"The coat suits you." He smiled, thinly. "You should keep it."

He played with an ivory cigarette holder as he explained his predicament. The Bear had been one of his most valued employees; he'd been essential to the smooth running of his operation. The Gentleman found himself in need of a replacement. A young man of his abilities could go far in this world; and he'd already proved himself, of course.

Seven years, was the offer. Seven years' service, and he'd live like a prince the whole time, and at the end of it, if he lived, he'd be packed off with enough money to see him right for the rest of his life.

There were odd requirements, of course. Not to say the Lord's Prayer, or to set foot in a church, until the term was up. Not even for Christmas, he was told, or for weddings. Why? Just think of it as one of the Gentleman's little peccadilloes, he was told. He was a God-fearing man, didn't feel it was right for thieves to go to Church if they weren't repentant. Plenty of time to look to your soul after you retire. It was strange, but far from the strangest thing you heard in London.

There was a written contract, of course.

He shrugged, reached the pen, looked for an inkwell. There was a flash of steel, a splash of red. He cradled his hand, looked up in confusion; the Gentleman met his eyes, calmly returning the blade to his sleeve, and smiled that cold smile again.

Mutely, he signed his name in blood.

***

He remembers.

***

May, 1924. The Rose and Crown again. Drinking alone again, glowering at the double handful of old soaks dotted around the bar at lunchtime. The great furry coat was draped on the seat next to him.

He was the Bear, now, feared and respected. He broke legs – or heads – for Sailor Jim, sometimes for the Gentleman's other dons; occasionally for the Gentleman himself. He'd presided over a couple of executions, in his time, including Jim's own brother; the man had been stealing from the don, and Jim couldn't face doing it himself.

No-one challenged him, or spoke over him; no-one even met his eyes.

Except little Alice Jones.

Old John Jones was the publican; he'd run this place since his own dad had died. He didn't always seem all that pleased at the dubious honour of Jim's patronage, but he didn't resist it much, either. As far as dons went, Jim wasn't all that dangerous, and he didn't usually allow stolen goods or the like into the pub itself.

Alice was sixteen, and was bright as sunlight, and

sweet as honey. Most of the regulars knew her; she'd been born and raised here, and even staying upstairs in the flat John shared with Molly, it was inevitable that she'd come out from time to time. And perhaps she'd seen how the old men were drinking themselves to death by degrees, and perhaps she'd seen how the young men were scarred, and had troubled heads, and brought a cloud of fear and violence in with them. But if she had, she hadn't showed it. She laughed with them, and listened to their stories, and played in the saloon bar, and she brought them a measure of happiness. And a year ago, she'd argued with her dad, and put her tiny foot down, and now she worked as a pot girl.

And as she'd grown into womanhood, she'd started flirting, and playing the coquette, and teasing the boys who came and went on Sailor Jim's business. And she never gave any of them her favours, but nobody smarted much from it.

He loved her.

He didn't want for the company of women – far from it – but she was the only girl he'd laid eyes on in years who didn't look at him with a little fear in her eyes, and didn't flinch when he looked at her in turn. And she was the only human being, man or woman, who showed him the least defiance.

And he loved her.

He knew – or he mostly knew – that she didn't love him in turn; that when she smiled at him, or laughed, or let her hand rest on his arm for just a moment, it meant nothing to her. That she was being friendly, and kind, in the unthinking way that only the truly innocent can be. Mostly, he knew that.

But he couldn't quite escape from the notion that she loved him too; that the reason she never gave any of the other boys the attention they wanted was that she wanted him in turn, and was waiting until she was old enough, until she could demand her father's approval for the match.

He berated himself for the fantasy. Of all his crimes – all the beatings, the killings, the terrible things he did in the Gentleman's name – only this gave him the slightest twinge of guilt. He didn't deserve her, it was unworthy to think of her in this way.

But even so, he loved her.

Alice came around the bar, collected the glasses, wiped the tables. A joke for one old wreck leaning on the bar, a squeal and a mock-slap for another. She reached his table, still laughing, and raised her eyebrows and winked at him as she worked. His heart lurched.

When his time was done, then. When his seven years were up, and he had his freedom, and he could set about putting his soul right, and earn the peace he felt he should want. Then he would speak to her, let her know his feelings, see how she felt in turn. She'd be twenty years old, by then.

***

H e remembers.

***

D ecember, 1926. He was in the front bar at the Rose and Crown, knocking back his fourth gin and grinding out his third cigarette. In another man, it might have seemed like nerves.

He was due to meet the Gentleman this evening, collect his final payment and put his affairs in order. The don had offered to extend his employment if he wanted, but the next contract was for life, and there are limits to what any man will do.

It had been a hard few years. His tally of kills had risen to twelve, in the end. He remembered them all. The beatings, the punishments – the men he'd hurt and crippled – he'd long lost count of; the faces blurred, fell into a ceaseless round of grimly banal brutality. But those twelve men remained sharp and clear in his mind, haunted his dreams. He didn't feel guilt – at least, nothing he recognised as guilt – but he was... aware of them. Counted them, obsessively, as though in a ledger he could never balance.

He'd not expected to miss church. He'd never been a religious man, even in the trenches; the incense and droning litany of his childhood had seemed as remote as the clouds, and as ephemeral. But as the seven years of his term had drawn on, as the blood drenched and stained him, the Masses his mother had dragged him to all those years ago had taken on a sacred quality, promised a peace he hadn't even realised he wanted.

The next day was a Sunday. Whatever he did next, he'd decided, he was going to church in the morning.

Every man in London knew his guilt. No warrant was ever issued for his arrest – that was the Gentleman's doing – but nobody had any illusions as to that. The Bear was a killer, many times over, and one day he'd swing for it.

In truth, it made his retirement a problem. With the end of his employment came the end of the Gentleman's protection. That, at least, he'd made clear. The next day, the police would be after him, not to mention a hundred other poor swine he'd trampled in his career, or who were hungry to make a name for themselves. He'd have to take the Gentleman's money and leave; up north, perhaps, or across the sea to France or Germany.

He drew out another cigarette, lit it, sucked at the smoke that seared his throat. He cast his eyes around the room again and shrugged. Even if not for the police and his many enemies, what was there to keep him here? He was hated and feared. The blood he'd shed, the violence in which he'd steeped himself, reeked from him. No man would take his hand; no man could treat him as a brother. Even his own brothers, now long since fled the country to Scotland and the Continent, terrified of what he'd become.

Alice came out from the kitchen to speak to her father, and his heart leapt in his chest. Something like actual pain clutched at him. He drew on his cigarette again, the tip flaring an angry orange as smoke curled around his head.

His dreams of her had died long ago. Now, when she looked at him, he saw the fear in her face, same as on everyone else's. She'd become cold to him; frightened. She was still the sweetest, kindest woman he knew, but she'd grown, shed some of her innocence, and she knew he was a monster now.

The day he'd seen that, he realised, was the day he'd started to dream of those he'd killed.

At twenty years of age, she was still unmarried, and hadn't even taken a sweetheart, that he knew of. But she was spending a fair amount of time with young Tom, who was Ernie's nephew, and it was supposed she would start stepping out with him soon.

His belly ached, roiling and sour, as he cast about irritably. The Gentleman hadn't told him when he'd see him, just that he'd see him that night. Just like the miserable fop.

There was Tom now, blowing in out of the cold and slamming the door shut behind him, stamping snow off his boots and cheerily greeting old John behind the bar.

Alice reached for a scarf, and he realised she was wearing a jacket. Set to head out, then. She smiled and waved at Tom, kissed her father on the cheek, and skipped over to the door. Tom opened it for her, and laid a hand on her elbow as they left.

He mused for a moment, then made up his mind. He stubbed out his cigarette, stood, and pulled on the great furry coat before following the young couple out into the night.

***

He remembers.

***

June, 1930. The men and women of the village of Saint-Jeanne knew well that the quiet man with the limp who owned and ran the pub was born in England. They knew that he was fleeing some terrible past, that Pierre DuMont was not his real name. They didn't care.

He'd come to Saint-Jeanne with a chestful of gold, it was said, and bought the tavern outright. He'd paid for the LeFevres' daughter to be sent to hospital in Paris when she'd fallen ill; he'd bought a house for Martin and

Charlotte Renard when they'd married in the spring. Half the families in the village owed him more than they could ever repay. He never asked for recompense, or even the slightest praise. And if he sometimes seemed troubled – if, in church, he prayed louder and more fervently than any other man there – then it was just as well, they said, that he'd come here to seek peace.

When little Alice Jones had discovered she was carrying her attacker's child, she'd taken one of the knives from the kitchen at the Rose and Crown and taken her own life. Her mother had followed soon after. He'd read about it in The Times, in a coffee house in Marseilles, three months after he'd left the country. "The Bear's Last Victims," the paper had called them.

For the first time since before the war, he'd cried. A man who'd survived the trenches, who'd murdered twelve men in cold blood, and he curled up on the floor of his hotel room and wept like a child, begging for forgiveness. From Alice, from God, from his mother.

He'd come out here. Tried to turn the Gentleman's money to good ends, to start to make amends for the harm he'd done. He'd prayed, he'd wept, he'd forced himself to relive every crime, every murder, every cruelty.

A year after he'd arrived, he'd gone to confession in the little church. Poor old Père Marcel had barely known what to do. They'd talked about him returning to England, to face justice; they'd talked about whether God's plan had brought him to Saint-Jeanne to find peace instead.

And slowly, painfully, he'd begun to heal.

And then, late one night in the summer of nineteen-thirty, old John Jones from the Rose and Crown had broken into the tavern and shot him in the chest.

Somehow the old man had found him, had tracked him to the sleepy village where he'd found sanctuary. He'd found his wife and daughter, dead by their own hands; he'd buried them. He'd lost everything, and the only thing that made sense had been to track down the man responsible and kill him. And now, four long years later, he'd succeeded. The former publican didn't even speak, didn't take a moment to gloat or to proclaim himself avenged. The moment he barged into the room, he raised his rifle and opened fire, and the Bear's life ended.

***

He feels a little fear, but mostly relief. And incredulity: three years of war and seven years as a criminal weren't able to kill him, but one old man with a rusty rifle did for him in a minute. He feels sadness, and regret, and the sure knowledge that he deserves this death. Gratitude, that God saw fit to give him time to repent before He took his life away.

There is light, and heat, and pain.

***

"I should have had you, really," says the Gentleman, carefully selecting a cigarette and sliding it into the end of his ivory holder.

He looks around him. He's in the Gentleman's room in the Rose and Crown again. He takes in the tattered rug, the battered mahogany desk, the faded prints on the wall.

"I – I don't –"

"It was a cinch, really. A brute like you? Seven years without church? You should be mine."

Silk and velvet rustle as he raises the holder to his lips and lights the cigarette; thin purple smoke circles his head.

He pats his chest, where the bullet struck him, but his shirt is unbroken and unstained. He looked up at his old employer.

"How did I get here?"

The Gentleman smiles thinly, in his way, leans back in his chair, and it strikes him that there's something wrong there. The man's proportions don't seem right: his arms and legs are too long, his back a little hunched. Why has he never noticed that?

The crime lord draws from his cigarette and elegantly flicks a little ash onto the floor. "That's the hell of it, if you'll excuse the term; you belong here. Not them. Little Alice Jones never said boo to a goose. Literally, in fact; did you know that? Although I don't think there were many geese in Hackney. Molly Jones was a kind, loving wife, and a fiercely devoted mother. Neither of them missed a single Sunday of church in her life. They deserve to go through there." He gestures with the cigarette holder. "Not you."

He looks over his shoulder at the door, turns back, frowns. "Am I in Hell?"

The Gentleman smirks. "You're in my rooms at the Rose and Crown. I've held you here for a moment before you go on. No Hell for you, my boy; you're confessed and shriven, and your contrition was heartfelt and genuine. That's the rules." He tuts, shakes his head. "I get them, I don't get you. That's His plan. How I wish it were the other way around. But you were never the target, my lad, much as you deserve to be. I've two souls for your one."

He stands, looks at the door behind him again. Looks back at the Gentleman. "Can I change places with them? If I go with you, will you let Alice and her mother go?"

The other man laughs, sets the cigarette holder down, leans forward with a leer. "If I could, dear boy, I wouldn't need you to offer. I don't enjoy my part in all this, you know. I don't like taking in good people who fall afoul of the rules, or letting bad people who get lucky go. But I'm not the Judge." He looks up.

"But why? That... it doesn't seem fair."

The Gentleman stands. "Perhaps you'd better tell Him that, when you see Him."

He turns and looks at the door again, turns back again. "I will."

The Gentleman smiles.

He walks to the door, opens it and steps out.

GRISEL

by Julius Horne

PART ONE

When people ask "were there really monsters?" they need to know the story of the boy, Grisel, and of how he kept the monsters at bay.

There was a time, long ago, when the monsters walked the land. Their evil kept them from the sunlight, it is true, but they freely stalked the shadows, intent upon trickery and foul deeds the like of which kept families in their homes at night, and small children in their beds.

Grisel though, was a boy with no bed to sleep in. He was an orphan abandoned, they say, because his pale and sickly face was unappealing. Repelled by the townsfolk, he kept to himself. His only sins those of being different, and of being all alone.

Forced to hide in the shadows—the very same shadows where the monsters lived—it is said that one of those monsters, an old trolless, took pity upon him. That or the taste of his flesh was as unappealing to the monsters as his appearance was to the people. Pity for a troll is not the same as it is for people. The old trolless needed a lookout for the daytime, and a worker for the night-time. When dusk came she would give Grisel tasks—climbing up and down the bridge to sweep it, to sift the pebbles, and to gather wish-pennies thrown from the bridge by lovers in the daytime—while she snuck off to find a juicy child to eat. Trolls, you see, love the taste of little children above all other things.

When the trolless slept, or ran out of chores, Grisel would be allowed to fish for food, and on rare occasions the boy would be seen on the outskirts of town, sat in his rags upon the arch of the bridge.

But Grisel was not a happy boy, and with sadness came spite. Each day he would remove a brick from the bridge. One by one they disappeared, so slowly that the old trolless never noticed, until a hole appeared. Through that hole the sun shone, burning the skin of the old trolless that slept beneath. Screaming with pain and anger, she fled from beneath the bridge to chide the boy, whereupon the midday sun completed its work, and she was turned to stone.

Fixing up the bridge, Grisel set about claiming it for his own, and there, with his rod and line, he would fish for his supper from dusk until dawn.

Trolls, though, will never let a good bridge go to waste. When news that the old trolless was now a moss-covered rock around which the river's current flowed, the younger trolls came to claim her home for themselves. Like the trolless before them, they found Grisel a paltry morsel unworthy of their attention, for he was not as plump and juicy as the children of the town, and he smelled as sickly as he looked. Chasing him away, they claimed the bridge, and Grisel moved on to the next, and the next, and the next.

"Why won't they let me alone?" He sighed, his feet

sore and weary. "All I want is a place of my own to sit and cast my line."

Travelling further afield, he followed the river into nearby woods, coming upon a fallen tree that crossed the water. Setting up as dusk approached, he settled down to fish. But soon the forest trolls appeared, and chased him from their land.

Moving up to higher ground, Grisel found rock pools among the mountain streams, and settled at a waterfall, and at dusk he started to fish.

"This is a good place for food," he said to himself. "Plenty of tasty fish and a big cave where I can sleep in the daytime."

Inside the big cave, he quickly discovered, lived a tribe of hungry mountain trolls. In no time at all he was forced to flee once more. Wherever he went, the trolls would come, until Grisel could no longer fish beyond the town walls.

Reluctantly, he crossed the bridge he used to fish, using the daytime to avoid the troll that lived there. Once inside, he begged for pennies on the street opposite the candy shop. But all the children of the town came past to get their treats, and none could spare a penny when a penny bought a sweet.

Of course Grisel had pennies of his own, the shiny wish-tokens gathered from the water beneath his bridge. Day by day they dwindled as he fed himself, until the day came when he had only a handful of pennies in his pocket. His tummy rumbled as he hatched a plan.

***

That night, just as he once climbed up and down his bridge, he climbed up to the roofs of the town, his rod and line in his hand. Sitting on the rooftop he baited his line—not with worms or maggots, but with as many sweeties as his last few pennies could buy—and he dangled his line before the open windows of the town's sleeping children.

He then tap-tap-tapped on the roof, loud enough to wake the slumbering children one by one, but quiet enough not to disturb their parents. On the streets below the watchmen went about their business without seeing a thing.

The children would wake, rub their eyes, and see a shiny sweetie dangling just within their reach, just outside their window. Was it a dream? Was it magic? Tired children don't think a lot, and one by one they reached for their prize.

One bit. Two bit. Three bit. They struggled, but Grisel was older and stronger, whisking them up and reeling them in, his club and his sack ready for his night's prize. Then, with a bulging sack, he shimmied down the walls, ran along the streets and off to his old bridge where a troll was waiting.

"Go away, Grisel!" Said the troll. "This bridge is mine!"

"Indeed, sir troll," Grisel replied. "But I just wish to pass. Let me pay a toll."

Giving over one of the babes to the hungry troll, Grisel went upon his way, along the river, through the forest, and up to the mountain waterfall. As he went he paid his toll in children, to the bridge trolls, and to the forest trolls until, at last, he arrived at the waterfall with but a single babe.

It was late. Dawn was coming. And with very few children in these parts, the trolls were hungry.

"Oh, mountain trolls!" He called. "I bring you a gift!"

"Who is it?" Said a gruff voice from within the waterfall cave.

"It is I, Grisel, the unappealing boy."

"What's yer gift?" The troll replied.

"Here! A fresh babe!" Grisel replied.

The sound of sniffing could be heard as Grisel unwrapped his gift, laying the sleeping babe upon a nearby rock.

"Come and get it!" He cried.

"We may be trolls," said the voice, "but we're not stupid! It's close to dawn and that rock will burn when the sun rises. Bring it closer."

"Well I'm not coming any closer," said Grisel, "show me a spot where the shade will protect you."

A thick troll finger poked out of the waterfall, pointing.

"There. Over there!"

"Very well," said Grisel, skipping down to the rock and laying the babe upon it. Stepping back, he watched as one, two, three trolls stepped out, scurrying down to the riverside as the morning sun rose into the sky. Protected by the mountain's shadow, the trolls scooped up their meal, and scuttled back into the waterfall.

***

Each day screams would awaken the town as the children were missed, and each night the watch would double, until all of the men were out protecting their babes. Each day Grisel would return to his old bridge, gather wish-pennies under the troll's watchful gaze, trade them for sweets from the candy shop, and then scuttle onto the roofs, pull out his rod, and fish for children.

With his job done he would pay his tolls and make his way to the mountain waterfall, where the last child would feed the tribe of trolls.

But that was not all that Grisel did. As the watch grew madder and stronger, he left clues at night and spread rumours in the day. It was the greedy troll under the bridge that took the babes, he whispered to any that would hear. As more children disappeared, the watchmen grew bolder, and angrier, until they surrounded the bridge, bearded the troll, dragging him with ropes out into the sunlight where he turned to stone.

Each morning after all the trolls were fed, Grisel would climb up above the mountain waterfall, and chip away a little rock, so slowly that the trolls never noticed.

With the bridge troll gone Grisel reclaimed his pitch, but after a short while returned to his fishing, and filled his sack anew. This time he had one fewer toll to pay, and upon reaching the mountain waterfall, had two babes to feed the trolls.

"Why are you so generous?" The troll chieftain asked, one day.

"I was brought up by an old trolless," replied Grisel. "It's my way of saying thank you."

***

As the weeks passed the watch spread its hunt for the babysnatchers, hearing whispers of the other bridge trolls, and then of the forest trolls that fed on screaming babes in the quiet of the night. Never did they suspect Grisel, the boy on the bridge, for he was weak, and sickly, and unworthy of their attention.

At last, the bridges were empty and the forests cleared. Grisel could visit the mountain waterfall with a full bag of babes, which he duly delivered to the spot beside the river. By now, of course, he had chipped away so much rock that his trap was ready to spring.

"Oh trolls!" He called. "I have your food!"

The crying babes made such a noise that not one, or two, or three trolls came from the cave, but the whole tribe. Scrambling down to the riverside, blissfully unaware that the mountain would offer no shade when the sun rose, they fell upon their food, eating up the babes on the spot. It was an indulgent feast for them, and they thought nothing of the sun as dawn broke and its light turned them, in an instant, to stone.

"Just as well," said Grisel, climbing up to the cave that would be his new home. "Those were the last children in town."

PART TWO

When people ask "what happened to the monsters?", they need to know the story of the man, once called Grisel, and how he made them disappear.

There was a time, not so long ago, when the monsters skulked in the barren places, far away from the eyes of men. Even at night they dared not appear, lest the rattle of their chains or the thumping of their feet attract the men who walked with lanterns and torches, with sticks and knives watching for the monsters while small children slept in their beds.

One town, its name spoken of only in hushed tones, had lost all its children to the monsters. All had gone within a few short months, and the watch had mournfully set about collecting their bones from the places—the bridges, the forest, the waterfalls—where they had been eaten by the monsters.

But no matter how thorough they were, many bones were missing, and many parents mourned without a grave to visit. It was a town bereft, and the search widened. There were trolls still out there, and it was agreed that the kingdom must be rid of them for its children to be safe.

Posters were put up all over the realm, offering a reward for the slaying of trolls, but try as they might, none of the self-appointed troll-slayers had the slightest idea of how to find, let alone slay, a troll. It came to pass that Grisel, a sickly old man who lived in a cave behind a mountain waterfall, came across just such a poster.

"A thousand marks?" He read. "That would give me something much better than a mountain cave to live in."

Pulling on his shabby coat, Grisel set off to the kingdom's capital, and there he set about spreading rumours.

"There is," he whispered to all who would listen, "a mountain kingdom ruled over by the largest, greatest troll of all. Only by finding and killing the king of the trolls shall the children be spared." He added, for good measure, that only a man called Grisel knew the whereabouts of the mountain kingdom.

News reached the ears of the king, who summoned Grisel to the Royal Palace. It was the grandest, shiniest, most magnificent building in all the kingdom, and Grisel said to himself, "Now this would be a nice place to live."

And so he met the king.

"You are the one called Grisel? Can you truly rid our kingdom of its trolls?"

"Indeed, your majesty," he said, bowing low. "My hatred for the trolls is so great that I have made it my duty to oppose them whenever they cross my path."

"And how would you do this?"

"Why give them what they desire, of course. Children."

"Children? You would have me give our children away? Impossible."

"Not all of them, your Majesty."

"It is for the children that I seek to cleanse the kingdom. What you suggest is unacceptable."

"They would not be harmed," said the old man, "and they would be returned to you. It is like catching fish. I need enough bait to feed all of the trolls, to lure them into the sunlight where they shall be turned to stone, never to trouble you again."

"I could do this without you," said the King. "Why should I agree to this?"

"Only I know the whereabouts of the great troll city that lies hidden deep within the mountains."

The king thought long and hard. It was a terrible decision, but he had no choice.

"Very well, I shall prepare an army to follow in your wake."

"An army? Oh no, there's no need. Just give me a cart, fill it with sweets, and leave the rest to me."

***

An hour before dawn the sweet-laden cart trundled through the city streets, the beckoning whisper of the old man enticing the children to follow. One by one they emerged from their houses, the sweet smell of candied fruits and chocolates casting its spell over them. Out of the city Grisel's cart trundled, and the children followed. Into the forests it went, a column of children gathering sweets as the old man cast them left and right, their shiny wrappers twinkling under the light of the setting moon.

Into a mountain pass they meandered as the moon passed behind the highest peak and the sweet cart descended into a dark tunnel. One by one the children paused, their fear of the dark overcoming their desire for confectionery.

"Where are we?" They asked as panic crept into their voices.

"Calm yourselves, children," said Grisel, "there are even more treats inside the mountain. More sweets, more cakes, more toys and more goodies than you have ever seen. Come gather them with me and you can take as much as you want back to your homes."

With a cheer the children cast away their fears, and ran merrily into the depths of the mountain.

***

Grisel returned alone with just a long face and an empty cart. Crowds parted as he made his way through the city and beyond the palace gates to the court of the king.

"The trolls are all dead," he said, "but so too are the children. It was tragic, I tried all that I could, but it was to no avail."

The shocked king stood, ashen faced, aghast.

"What happened?"

"We arrived too soon. The trolls poured out of the mountain and descended upon the children, tearing them apart, devouring them limb by limb as the moon sank beyond the horizon. Even the great troll king was there, feasting. Alas, no child survived, but the trolls were so gorged by human flesh they failed to see the sun come up, and every last monster was turned to stone."

"Every last one?" The king sank to his knees. Even as he realised what he had done he heard the sounds of the people beyond the palace. The fathers, the mothers, the sisters, the brothers. All baying for blood. Not for the blood of Grisel, but for the king, whose remorseful flight through the corridors of power could not escape the vengeful citizens who found their mark and, like the trolls had done with their children, tore him limb from limb.

Grisel, meanwhile, covetously eyed the palace court.

"This," he said to himself, "will do nicely."

***

B ut what really happened to the monsters?

Only Grisel knew. Swift to claim his reward before chaos made the kingdom a republic, he returned to the mountain, and to the city of the trolls. There, at the cave mouth, there were no petrified monsters, and he pressed on to the troll king's court. It was a dark and grim place filled with scattered sweet wrappers and the tangled bones of little boys and girls. As Grisel entered the Royal Chamber, the troll king sat, munching on the leg of a boy, surrounded by mountains of wish-pennies gathered from the the troll tithes that gave him power.

"Welcome back, Grisel. What news of the king and his army?"

"They believe you dead, your majesty," the old man said, bowing low. "And now, with your help, you can feast on as many children as you want, and they shall never know."

"And how would you do this?"

"There will always be poor, and sick and unwanted children. With my Royal reward and the wish-penny horde you promised, I shall return to build orphanages—the Royal Palace shall be the first—to care for these poor waifs and strays."

"Care? Why should you care for them?"

"To keep them fresh and plump and juicy, your majesty. To keep your larders stocked with no need to use bridges to hide from the daylight. I shall bring them here, and you shall be fed for all time."

The troll king laughed, a deal was struck, and the monsters lived happily—and profitably—ever after.

THE MOUSE, THE BIRD AND THE SAUSAGE

by Kirstin Fulton

Once upon a time, there was a mouse, a bird and a sausage (yep, a sausage) who put their heads together on a great idea.

"I've been flying around solo for too long," the bird bowed his head to a motley pair of friends. "I'm handy and fast, and all the other birds seem to resent me for it. I wish so much for some true friends and a warm, cozy cosy place to call home."

"I know just how you feel," cried the mouse. "Years of pilfering nibbles and sneaking through dusty passages is sure making me gloomy. And all my brothers and friends died in that crazy circus stunt last year. I am so so lonely!" Fat, salty tears rolled down from his whiskers and dripped to the floor.

"Don't cry, dear Mouse," replied the sausage, bent over in emotion. His guts ached when people around him cried. "Life's been a dull plight without my sausage family. Just weeks ago, they were packed off to the stadium where I'm sure they were sizzled and slathered in sauce before being guzzled by fat fanatics. I couldn't stand the thought of being gobbled up by piggish people like that, so I wriggled out of the butcher's fingers and escaped. But now I wish I hadn't. I am a woeful sausage!"

And all three sat in a sombre circle for moments until bird - who was the only one of them with a brain for strategy - came up with an ingenious idea.

"Say!" he cried. "Let's live together! We can have a little house just for us, and we shall be best friends."

"Yes!" Mouse chimed in. "We will all have our own tasks. It will be super!"

"Fantastic!" said Sausage. "But I'm no good at anything at all. I don't even have arms! What can I do to help make a good home?"

"I'll think of something," Bird crooned.

And he did.

Some time passed and the three odd fellows set up a grand system. Bird, who was indeed handy, set to gathering wood every day. Mouse, who was a great homemaker - as most mice are – fetched water, kept a fire going, and set a glorious table every night. And Sausage, in all his unfortunate corporal limitations, cooked food for his friends. This was the perfect task for he could smash, press and beat any food into the perfect shape and texture.

It was a well-oiled machine.

One day while out gathering, Bird ran into a raucous birdie pack.

"Hey there!" a big red bird snapped. "Where've you been for so long?" A whole horde of beady black eyes set on Bird, and he felt his quills prick up.

"Uhh," he replied slowly. "I have set up a nice company with some new friends. We each have our own tasks and it is a most comfortable living arrangement."

The giant red bird cocked his head sharply to the side. Curious, he studied Bird for a moment then asked, "And what task is yours?"

Bird let out a deep breath, and felt surprised that he'd been holding it. He explained how he was the gatherer and spent his day in the forest, while the others stayed at home and did homely things.

"Bahhhh ha ha!" cried the flock.

"Fool!" shouted a small, tawny sparrow with a cracked bill.

"Sucker!" howled another, a woodpecker (who had always been a jerk).

"You mean to say," said the red bird, "that you haul and lift all day while those layabouts soak up the warmth of your fire and take naps all day? You're a real sad sack, Bird. You deserve those loafers."

A whirlwind of cackling laughter surrounded Bird, then slowly lifted from the downy patch of grass and left him sitting alone. He dipped his head low and sang himself a sad song before taking off back home.

In the little house, Mouse and Sausage were happy to see Bird return.

"Yay, Bird!" called Mouse, "Have a seat. Dinner is near ready."

Bird sat glumly down, while Sausage hooked his serving cap on and attached a platter of roasted nuts and vegetables. (No meat, for obvious reasons.) He twirled over to the group and laid the platter down on the well laid table.

The three gobbled in silence until Bird suddenly erupted. "Listen!" he bellowed.

Mouse nearly shot through the roof. "Great beans, Bird, what is it?!" he shouted. "You nearly caused my heart to explode!"

"I've had a good think, and I believe that I'm being taken advantage of here for my brute strength, keen eyes and general handiness. I think we should reassign the household tasks. From now on, I will stay in the warmth of the cottage while you two will lift and haul."

Confusion and discomfort washed over the faces of Mouse and Sausage. After the shock subsided, they both started rambling at once.

"But why, Bird?" wondered Sausage. "Everything works so nicely this way. And you know that I can't lift and haul. I have no arms for Pete's sake! Bahhhh!" Sausage cried into his plate. He had been so happy to finally have a task worthy of him.

"Oh, Bird," grumbled Mouse, "I am disappointed. You know the outside world threatens us in many more ways that it threatens you. Why would you want to put us in harm's way?"

But Bird would not listen to his friends. Were they

even really his friends, he wondered. They just made him into a pack mule. The laughter of the bird community rang bitterly in his ears. Shaking it from his head, he stared back at the two in silence.

"It's not up for debate. I'm in charge here and this is how it will be from now on." And Bird proceeded to reassign tasks. His would now be to bring water, while Mouse's was to cook. Sausage - much to his horror - had to fetch wood.

The next morning they set upon their new routine. The wood supply was running low, so Sausage snuggled into a pair of trousers and a thick hat. Hopping into the yard, a cold gust of air caught his breath and carried it clean away. "Oh my!" he choked. This was going to be leagues more uncomfortable than sitting by the hearth watching soup bubble. Maybe Bird is right, he thought. Maybe we have taken advantage of him, sending him out into the cold every day.

"Sausage," a voice squeaked behind him. "Be careful! Just gather wood and come straight back." Mouse was worried for Sausage. He didn't have much in the way of brains. Only remnants of brains, really - so he often got caught in sticky situations. It's a wonder he'd made it this far in life.

Sausage nodded at his friend and shifted off down the path into the thick, mossy wood.

And that was the last anyone saw of Sausage.

Well, except for Dog who met Sausage quite soon into his journey. Dog was a jolly beast with a thick pink tongue that dangled unabashedly to his front paws. Today, like every day before, Dog was guarding the forest path against thieves and spies. It was a good job for him, as he got to sit all day and sniff out travellers. And sniffing the dirty parts of beasts and men was his absolute favorite thing. But he was old and his instinct had left him. Nowadays, thieves and spies not only evaded the guard dog, but often tricked him into helping with their cunning plans. While any tendency to assault and maul he reserved for little old ladies, children, and as it turns out, earnest sausages.

Sausage whistled his way through the forest, trying to keep his lips from freezing shut, when suddenly a massive puff of white fur loomed before him, blocking the path.

"Whaddaya doin' in these parts?!" shouted Dog. A gust of foul air rushed from his throat and knocked Sausage clean over.

"Ah!" squealed Sausage, rolling on the ground. "Ah!" He was hysterical.

Dog approached him and sucked in a great sniff of scent. This caused Sausage to slightly hover in the air, which practically paralyzed him with fear. Dog, however, was very pleased by Sausage's aroma and set his mind to question him thoroughly, as all guard dogs should.

"Asked you a question, I did! Whaddaya doin' on my path?" Dog snarled.

"Your path?! So sorry, Dog sir. I didn't... I didn't know it was your path!" If Sausage could wet himself, he would have then, so terrified he was of the giant mongrel. "I'm just gathering wood for our cottage, sir!"

"Spy!" cried Dog. "Sausages don't gather wood! They have no arms to gather! You are most certainly a spy. Who sent ya?" His mouth was salivating wildly now.

Sausage's eyes bugged out of his crispy skin. Why would anyone spy on a dirty old dog? Don't ask that, he told himself. But before he even had a chance, Dog lapped him up with his soggy tongue and swallowed him in one great gulp.

And that was really the last anyone saw of Sausage.

That evening, Bird and Mouse were worried for their friend. He had been gone for hours. Bird sat glumly by the fire while Mouse paced across the wooden floor, wringing his small paws. Finally, he spoke up.

"This is your fault, Bird! You wanted us to do work that is not suited for us, and look what happens. Sausage is lost or squirreled away in the nest of some evil beast. You must go find him."

Bird pointed a shiny eye in Mouse's direction and without a word, he walked out.

It didn't take long for Bird to spot a mangy dog lying on the main path. He must have seen Sausage, bird thought.

He swooped down and sat beside the dog's muddy face. The beast was sleeping contently, whimpering slightly through some colourful dream.

"Hey there!" shouted Bird. Dog jumped straight out of his peaceful rest and growled at the little creature.

"Hey there, Dog," Bird continued, graciously

ignoring Dog's deep rumbling. "Do tell me, have you seen a cheeky Sausage scamper by here. He would have been wearing a ridiculous fat cap and pants that miraculously stay on somehow."

"Sausage?" he sneered, "Well yesssss, I saw a filthy little sausage. Spy he was! Gobbled him whole. Tasty little spy. Expect he's goo in my guts by now." And to prove it, Dog belched loudly in Bird's face.

Bird was stunned. Gobbled?! What would he tell Mouse? "Murderer!" he cried. "You killed our sweet and earnest Sausage!"

"Nonsense!" bellowed Dog. "He was not sweet--quiet spicy, really. And he was a slimy little spy. Said he was gathering wood. And whoever heard of a sausage doing such a thing? Sausages should be at the hearth, pushing a pot. Not in the wilderness."

Bird's wings were filled with lead and he struggled to lift himself into the air and home to Mouse.

Mouse wept bitterly when he heard the news. "Our poor simple Sausage!" he cried. "He didn't deserve such a grisly fate. He should have spent the rest of his days here helping with our food."

Bird nodded without uttering a word. The two agreed with heavy hearts that they would keep up their happy home best they could, just the two of them.

By that time they were both famished. Bird spread out the table carefully, while Mouse headed for the kitchen to get the food.

Some time passed and Mouse was still in the kitchen. Bird became impatient. "Everything is set and ready!" he called to Mouse. "How is the soup coming?" But there was no response.

"Hey-o! Mousey? Where are you? I've got a cracking hunger for some soup!" But again, nothing.

This made Bird a bit nervous. Was Mouse losing his hearing? Had he snuck out and left Bird all alone? Oh! To be abandoned by a mouse and a sausage in one day, that would be the ultimate shame.

He quietly walked into the kitchen and called out. But there was no Mouse. Well, there was a mouse, but by now his lungs were full of scalding soup and he was roasting away in the bottom of the pot, having plunged to his death. Unaccustomed to the giant ladle and pot, Mouse had toppled in the moment he tried to serve dinner.

"Mouse?" cried Bird again. Frantically, he searched amongst the woodpile, tossing sticks aside in case his friend had become trapped. As he hunted, Bird didn't notice that some of the wood had ended up near the hearth, and had caught fire. Suddenly, thick smoke filled the room.

"Ah!" he coughed. "Oh my!" He rushed out to the well to gather water and painfully cranked up the bucket. Bird wings are not well suited for turning a crank, so it took him an agonizingly long time to pull the bucket towards him, and his feathers caught in the thick rope.

"Oh, good grief!" he cried, struggling against the rope. Full, the bucket teetered on the edge. With a crash, Bird's struggles with the rope sent it spinning back down the shaft.

The rope snapped taut and Bird, who was by now good and tangled, was yanked from his feet and plummeted down the well.

And you see, some birds don't swim. As he fought the water from closing over his head, Bird wished he were high in the air collecting twigs and breathing the crisp forest breeze. And that image of happy gathering was the last he saw before the world went dark.

ONCE UPON A TIME

by Leland Thoburn

"Off with her head." The Queen scowled and pointed her bony finger at the flower girl who had just dropped a rose. Nobody moved.

"Off with her head, I command you!" the Queen shrieked. Black hair streaked with grey fell across her face.

"Now dear…" The King slouched in his throne, picking at a fingernail.

"Don't you 'now dear' me." Queen Cinderella brushed back her hair and spun around.

The King waved absently to the flower girl who stood still, frozen in fear. "You may go, dear." The little girl dropped her remaining flowers and ran, crying, from the room.

"Off with your head, then."

"You can't, I'm the King." Traces of irritation began to cut their way through his boredom.

Cinderella turned away and clenched her teeth. "King Charming, my ass. King Flatus would be more like it."

A small, chinless man entered the room. He carried

rolls and sheets of paper, some of which fell to the floor as he looked around at the guards. Then, he trotted towards the thrones. He stopped in front of the Queen and pushed his spectacles up on his nose.

"I don't recall sending for the royal accountant," said the King.

The little man looked nervously towards the Queen.

"I did, you buffoon. I'm going to Paris. Alone." She emphasized the last word bitterly, and then turned and smiled sweetly at the accountant. "How soon will the funds be available?"

"All the reserves are gone, your Majesty."

Cinderella scowled. "Borrow."

"The World Bank won't accept any more IOUs."

"Off with their heads."

"That would be an act of war," sighed the King.

"And your point is?" Cinderella demanded.

"We had to dismiss the army last week," the King said, sitting up. The accountant nodded as he again pushed his spectacles back up his nose.

"Raise taxes on the rich," Cinderella ordered.

"The last one declared bankruptcy three weeks ago," stated the King.

"Raise taxes on the middle class."

"There aren't any of them left either."

"Then tax the peasants."

"The tax rate is already 110%."

Cinderella looked around as if searching for someone to behead. "Levy an estate tax, a value added tax, a sales tax, a property tax, an alternative minimum tax, a use tax, anything. There must be some way to raise money."

"Nobody has any money left." The King resumed his picking.

"Throw them in jail if they won't pay."

"We jailed the last peasant on Wednesday." He held his fingernail up to the light and studied it.

Cinderella turned her scowl back to the accountant. The ferocity of her glare startled him into dropping his remaining papers. She jabbed her finger at him and screamed. "Off with his head." The accountant fell to his knees, while the guards paused and looked to the King. He yawned and waved absently. The two largest guards grabbed the accountant and dragged him, kicking and pleading, out of the chamber.

Cinderella turned to the King. "If you truly loved me forever after you'd send me to Paris."

The King lowered his head into his hands. "I should have married Snow White," he mumbled under his breath.

***

A gloom hung over the Merry Kingdom. The castle, which stood on top of a hill, brooded over the landscape like a gargoyle. The roads were empty, and all of the shops were shuttered. The furtive figure of a tax collector darted, ninja-like, cursing, from empty house to empty house. Nothing else stirred.

Almost nothing.

Outside the castle, a dwarf crouched, listening, as still and silent as only a dwarf trained in the ancient arts can be. In the distance, a church bell tolled midnight. The dwarf touched the tip of a dagger to his tongue, tasted blood, and spat. "Soon, my precious, soon," he whispered as he turned and slipped away into the woods.

Two hours later, the dwarf scuttled up a ridge, turned and stared at the woods behind. Satisfied he was alone, he dropped down into a shadowy, mist-filled valley, from which the howl of a far-off wolf was the only sound. He reached a clearing where he waited, motionless, knowing that any wrong move now would be his last. Nearby, someone, or something, whistled a refrain of "Whistle While You Work." He whistled back in kind, and waited.

Another dwarf appeared from around a boulder. "Come. She-who-must-be-obeyed is waiting." The two shadow warriors melted into the night.

***

Once it had been known as Happy Valley. No longer. The last vestige of the King's authority disappeared two years ago when one of the King's hunters entered the valley in pursuit a wounded deer. Eventually, the doe emerged. Not so the hunter.

Nestled in a far corner of the valley lay a small cottage. Once it had been a gay cottage, filled with happy days and comforting nights. Now, trees leaned over it like brooding assassins, and encroaching ivy pinned open its broken shutters. The trophy head of the King's hunter stared down from a mount above the door. Even the moon feared to enter this darkened hollow. The only light came from a small campfire that sputtered more smoke than flame.

"You took long enough." The dwarf held his hat in his hands and looked straight ahead at the source of the reprimand. A small woman moved into view at the edge of the firelight. Twin bandoliers crossed her ample bosom, and a bloodied headband held raven locks back from her piercing blue eyes. She stood, arms akimbo, the blush on her cheeks flaring in the firelight. "What did you learn?"

"The army has been dismissed. The kingdom is bankrupt. All of the citizens are in jail."

A smile crept on to Snow White's lips. Wider it grew, until her face split with laughter. The dwarf watched, fearful, for he had never seen her amused before. "Excellent," she said when she regained her composure. "Our time is at hand. Come quickly." She raised her fingers to her lips and pierced the night air with a whistle that sounded more like the hunting cry of an eagle than anything human. Soon, the glade in front of the cottage filled with dwarves, fawns, a rabbit, a puppy and a skunk. Snow White faced the multitude. Her shrill, chirpy voice sundered the gloom like a sword.

"'Vengeance shall be mine,' saith the Lord, and we are indeed the righteous tools of His almighty wrath. To council!" she shouted and led the multitude into the cottage.

A long table dominated the room. The dwarves sat, their long noses and fiercely scowling eyes peering above the thick, oaken tabletop. The animals all found places around the room to stand or squat. Snow White sat in a large, carved wooden chair at the head of the table. When all were settled, she called roll.

"Angry, Nasty, Psycho, Deadly, Sickly, Ugly, Attorney." Each of the seven dwarves answered when his name was called.

"Bombi, Stomper, Fouline, Flayer, Cerberus." Each of the animals, likewise, responded.

Satisfied, Snow White stood, her presence growing larger as if by her will alone. "Tonight is the night," she announced. "Tonight, we take back the Merry Kingdom, in the name of the people." She pounded the table. Cheers rang out from every corner.

"Stomper!" Snow White called out over the cheers. A sour-looking rabbit emerged from the crowd. Both of his ears were nicked, and a crimson scar ran across his face, terminating at a mutilated eye. He peered up at Snow White with his one good eye and slammed his foot on the ground.

"I want you and the other animals to remain behind and protect against counter attack," she told him. The rabbit's head drooped, and a tear came to his eye. A smile of affection spread across Snow White's face. "What's the matter my little love bunny?" she cooed. The rabbit looked up.

"I want to kill," he hissed.

As if on cue, the dwarves began chanting, "kill, kill, kill…" Soon the animals joined in, hopping about and shouting, "kill, kill, kill." Snow White stood on her chair, waving her arms and trying in vain to regain control. The din was silenced only when the skunk – who had a habit of becoming excited at times like this – lost control and sprayed the dwarf known as Attorney.

With a scraping of chairs and a clatter of hoof and clog, the cottage quickly emptied. Last to leave was the freshly befouled dwarf, who emerged, stumbling, muttering and cursing. He turned to face the crowd, which kept its distance. He raised his voice. "Please, listen to me. Revolution carries with it great risk. You could be hurt, maimed, killed, or included in a commercialized version of a fairy tale for children. These are grave risks for which Snow White will not be held liable. You must each sign a waiver…"

Attorney flourished his sheaf of papers, while the dwarves and animals grumbled and backed up, keeping their distance. Snow White stepped forward, waving her hands.

"Everybody, stop." They did. She turned to Attorney. "You spineless moron."

"But I only…"

"Off with his head!" she shouted, and a cheering mob of animals and dwarves pounced on the protesting dwarf and dragged him away, screaming, into the darkness.

"Snow White and the six dwarves, hmmm, not so good," she mused to herself as she sat, alone in the clearing, trying to count to six on her fingers.

Soon, the dwarves and animals returned. All except for Attorney. Fresh stains darkened fur and tunic alike, and blood dripped from the mouth of Cerberus, the puppy. All wore a smile. For them, the night's festivities had begun.

***

"Mirror, mirror, on the wall, who's the fairest of them all?" Cinderella looked up, smiling, at a shattered mirror that hung crookedly on the wall of her bedroom.

"It can't hear you anymore. You killed it," stated Fairy Godmother, who lay on the floor, chained and bound.

Cinderella spun savagely. "Silence!" she screamed.

"Listen, sweetie…" Fairy Godmother began. Before she could finish, Cinderella knelt down and slapped tape across her mouth.

"I am keeping you alive for one purpose and one purpose only. Do you understand?" Fairy Godmother squirmed as Cinderella tightened the ropes around her legs. "Do you understand?" demanded Cinderella.

Fairy Godmother winced and slowly, painfully, defiantly, shook her head.

Cinderella leapt up, removed a sword from the wall, and swung. The blade cleaved space, stopping inches from Fairy Godmother's neck.

"Do you understand?" Shrieked Cinderella, holding the sword quivering in her hands.

Fairy Godmother nodded, her eyes wide with terror. Cinderella rested the tip of the sword on the floor and leaned forward, towering over the old pixie.

"Now, about the money for Paris. I have a wish…" Tears formed in the corners of Fairy Godmother's eyes as Cinderella began detailing her budgetary needs. Suddenly, from outside in the hall, a blood curdling scream stopped Cinderella mid spittle. She jerked around just as the door to the bedchamber slammed open. There, on the threshold, stood Snow White, legs spread wide, hands gripping a nicked and bloodied blade.

"Death to the oppressor," she shouted. Her grim intentions shone through the grime and blood on her face. Fairy Godmother quickly rolled into a darkened corner, out of harm's way.

Cinderella smiled. "Would pretty little strumpet like a nice, shiny, red apple, hmmm?"

Show White raised her sword and waited.

"No, I suppose not," Cinderella said, lifting her sword and facing her nemesis. "Then die, despicable ditz." Cinderella swung with all her might, while Snow White skipped deftly aside and watched, as steel sparked against stone.

"Wretched gammer, you shall deregulate or perish." Snow White swung her sword in a deadly arc, only to watch it deflect off a stone pillar behind which Cinderella had ducked.

"Your rabble are no match for my bureaucrats, vertiginous slut," growled Cinderella, emerging back into the open.

The fight roared on. Before each attack, the warriors took pains to announce the particular political agenda that drove their fury.

"Higher taxes provide more government services, filthy chippy," shouted Cinderella.

"Less government regulation of private enterprise encourages growth, foul termagant," snarled Snow White.

Thrust and parry, parry and thrust. Blade against blade. The two combatants slung steel, aphorisms and insults at each other for hours, only to find their best blows countered with the grimmest of determination.

"Oh goody, a catfight." Hearing the commotion, King Charming had entered the room and was sitting in a chair, watching, as the two fighters rained blow after blow and platitude after platitude on each other. "If this is about me, there's no need to fight. There's plenty of 'charm' to go around, if you know what I mean. Now sing after me, ladies, 'Someday, my prince will come...'"

Cinderella and Snow White stopped fighting, looked at each other, and nodded. In an instant, two blades clove the breast of the King, who writhed, twitched once, and sagged dead, impaled on the chair like an insect on a tray.

The disarmed warriors flopped into chairs, grateful for any moment's respite that would permit rejuvenation of their tortured limbs. As they sat, gasping, a muffled cry rose from the corner of the room.

Fairy Godmother rolled into view, coming to rest at the feet of Snow White. Her face was blue and her chest heaved in spasms. Snow White tore the tape off her mouth, and Fairy Godmother wheezed and gulped for air. "You shouldn't do that to a mouth-breather," she said when she had caught her breath. Snow White loosened her bindings, and Fairy Godmother fluttered, hovering, into the center of the room. Only the faintest trace of blue remained. "You know, sweeties, I have an idea."

The two belligerents stood, looking at each other warily, and then at Fairy Godmother.

"You could go on like this forever, and for what? Neither of you can win. You're too evenly matched."

Snow White grinned. "Like hell," she said, rocking Cinderella with a right cross. Cinderella promptly returned the blow with feeling.

"Wait, wait," Fairy Godmother shouted, interjecting her tiny body in the midst of the melee. "God forbid one of you should win, what does that buy you? Constant fear of revolution and assassination, not knowing from whence the next blow might fall. Is that what you want?"

They shook their heads.

"So, here's my plan. We'll let everyone think you're deathly opposed to each other, like dwarves and hunters; they've been at it for centuries. The citizens will pick sides and every four years they'll vote. They'll think they have a choice, but no matter who wins we'll tax, spend, and regulate them into slavery. Meanwhile, we'll live like kings." They all three looked at King Charming, who was stiffening in his chair. "Like queens," Fairy Godmother corrected.

"Share power with this execrable harpy? Not on your life," Snow White said, stomping on Cinderella's foot.

"Dwarf doxy here can't even govern her way out of

the sack," replied Cinderella as she slapped Snow White's face.

The two women clinched and grappled, pulling hair, biting, and kicking until they fell, exhausted, to the floor.

"My darlings, wait, listen to me." Fairy Godmother flitted about in the utmost anxiety. "You can have power and share it too. Two seemingly opposed forces locked in stalemate make a far more stable base of power than any single tyrant can ever achieve."

Cinderella was the first to grasp the idea. "Vile harlot, don't you realize that nobody will revolt as long as they think they have a choice?" she said, kicking Snow White in the shin.

Fairy Godmother nodded approvingly.

Pain melted off Snow White's face as comprehension dawned. "Loathsome virago, I understand better than you that if we consolidate power we can turn the Merry Kingdom into an oligarchy the likes of which the world has never seen," she said, twisting Cinderella's ear.

"Now you've got it!" shouted Fairy Godmother. Snow White eyed Cinderella warily as they both arose, while Cinderella for her part cautiously assessed her opponent in a new light. Slowly, their grim faces relaxed, and smiles replaced frowns. Fairy Godmother beamed.

Soon, the revolution ended. Life returned to normal in the Merry Kingdom. The dwarves hated the hunters; the hunters hated the dwarves. Every four years they took it out on each other in hard-fought elections that shifted power like clockwork, and with it, the hopes and dreams of the realm. On and on it went, year after year, while for the deer, skunks, rabbits, puppies and flower girls, nothing ever really changed.

And they all lived happily ever after.

THE END

THE FRAG PRINCE

by Andrew K Lawston

It was just after lunch one fine Monday afternoon when Prince Bouffard wandered out of the palace to search for Tuesday with a spherical handheld multiscan. After three generations of his family using the asteroid as a frag production plant, the atmosphere was pretty stable, so Bouffard didn't even think to switch on his re-breather as he stepped into the dusty exterior.

Within minutes he had reached the top of a small hill, and gazed out over the raw, pocked surface that comprised his mother's asteroid kingdom. The landscape was flat and drab, broken only by the occasional crater, and by the blowholes: vents where excess heat created by the frag production department was periodically displaced into the atmosphere through jets of high pressure, super-heated steam.

They had all combed the palace for Tuesday, and had ransacked the philosophy section of the extensive royal library to see how such a thing as a day could ever be lost. They'd been looking for so long that Bouffard realised the answer must surely lie outside; in the flat red expanse of rock that formed nine tenths of his home world, Viard. Perhaps even as far away as Viard City, the rough settlement at the South Pole where most of their hundred thousand subjects lived and traded with the other populated asteroids.

With no particular destination in mind, Prince Bouffard set off towards a blowhole, idly tossing the multiscan from hand to hand as he trudged across the desolate landscape.

He'd only been walking for ten minutes when, to his delight, the scanner bleeped, indicating either a temporal distortion or a prompt to recharge the unit. Bouffard raced forward towards the blowhole, tossing the multiscan into the air with a whoop of joy, already imagining his parents' proud faces when he found Tuesday.

The multiscan soared into the air ahead of Bouffard, unfettered by the grav boots that kept him tethered close to the ground. As it flashed towards the sky, the Prince skidded to a halt, terrified he'd thrown it hard enough to send the thing into orbit; gradually the distant shape slowed, peaked, and began to descend in a leisurely arc.

Bouffard knew it would take more than a fall of a few dozen metres to damage the robust industrial scanner, but jogged on to retrieve it in any case, ignoring the pain in his feet that troubled him whenever he ran.

To his horror, however, the scanner floated gently into the blowhole. Bouffard had nearly closed the distance and thought he could catch the bleeping sphere, but just as he reached the shaft, a powerful jet of scalding steam erupted into the air, and the multiscan was lost into the depths of the hollow asteroid. There was no air down there, he knew, and with the frag production plant almost entirely automated, no chance of asking any friendly worker to retrieve it for him.

He'd hoped to prove himself a hero, but now Prince Bouffard could only sit by the blowhole and sigh heavily.

But then, a voice in the wilderness. "What's the matter, my prince?"

Bouffard's head whipped round to find the owner of the voice, but saw only an unprimed frag undulating around the blowhole, probably drawn to the heat. It looked like a pale slug, but its pink hide was dotted, of course, with human pores, fine hairs and even the odd pathetic nipple.

The Prince sighed again. "Sometimes I wish I was a frag," he said, "and could just wander around mindlessly with no worries about lost Tuesdays and multiscans."

There was a pause. "Ah, so that was your scanner that fell in the blowhole? Tough break."

This time Bouffard was certain. The Frag hadn't moved, but the voice had definitely come from somewhere in its amorphous body. A smooth neutral voice, genderless but pleasant.

His parents were kind to the unprimed frags, letting the mindless, raw organic material roam free until they were needed for a battle and they could be imprinted with the memories, training and physical prowess of the system's greatest soldiers. Cheap, plentiful, and utterly expendable. He'd never heard of an unprimed frag being able to speak, however.

It spoke again. "Of course, I don't breathe yet, and a bit of steam won't bother me much. I could probably fish it out if you want?"

Bouffard's excitement overcame his suspicion at the Frag's voice. "Could you? It would save me a great deal of embarrassment!"

The Frag squelched up to the lip of the blowhole's shaft, and appeared to lean forward as though it could peer into the blackness. "It's not too deep. I could get it. You'll have to make it worth my while, of course."

"Oh, of course," agreed the Prince, jumping to his feet with glee. "What could a frag possibly want, though?"

"I tell you what, if I get your scanner for you, how about you take me back to the palace for the night? That'd be pretty cool, for a frag. I could eat dinner with you, sleep on your bed... no funny business, just like a sleepover!"

Prince Bouffard contemplated the shapeless lump of flesh before him and felt ill at the thought of it spread over his luxurious four poster bed. But there were ways and means around this sort of bargain.

"Of course," he lied. "I accept!"

Without another word, the Frag toppled itself over the lip of the blowhole, and disappeared from view. Prince Bouffard waited patiently for several minutes, but could hear or see nothing.

Just as he was about to call out to the Frag, there was a brief rumble and another immense jet of scalding steam burst from the shaft.

Bouffard sank to his knees on the dusty rock, certain he'd lost his last chance of retrieving the palace's last multiscan unit. Even the majestic sight of the asteroid belt looming over him in the afternoon sky couldn't cheer him. His mother the Queen was going to be so disappointed, and he couldn't blame her. He'd behaved like an excited child who couldn't look after his toys.

"Sorry for the wait, my prince. It was a bit further down than I thought, and a bit stuck." With those words, and a little popping noise, the multiscan bounced out from the blowhole and rolled to the Prince's feet. He snatched it up with delight, just as the Frag began to haul itself from the shaft.

"Thanks!" shouted Prince Bouffard as he turned and ran full pelt back towards the palace.

The Frag shouted after him. "Hey, slow down! I've got no legs and even at full wobble speed I'll never keep up with you!"

Never mind, my fraggy friend, thought the prince. Tomorrow you'll be rounded up, primed, and sent to the front line. And no one need ever know.

***

When he returned to the palace, he realised his trip had taken longer than he thought. The housedroids had set the banqueting hall's great table for dinner and the Queen was already seated in her finest emerald gown.

She raised an amused eyebrow at his clumsy bow, and waited until he had sat down and helped himself to a hummingbird samosa before speaking.

"So. Did you find Tuesday?"

Bouffard blushed, though he would have loved to know what his mother had been doing in their palace while he'd been running around on the arid plains. He'd been told it was modelled on Versailles, although he had no idea what that was. The rest of the asteroid seemed to have been modelled on a Dorset quarry. "Not yet," he said, "but the answer must be out there on the plains. I had a signal from the multiscan."

He held out the spherical unit, but a housedroid intervened, and took it to the Queen at the other end of the long dining table. The Queen took the multiscan eagerly, and even pushed her spectacles up her nose to concentrate, but then sighed.

"It was bleeping because it's run out of charge, dear."

"Ah."

With that, they began to eat. The King wandered in a little later, having dozed off in the library. They were tucking into their starters when suddenly there was a loud knock at the door.

The Queen threw down her fork in annoyance. "Oh, what a nuisance! You fly to a tiny asteroid in a distant solar system to farm genetically superior super soldiers, and you still can't get through a meal without a bloody cold caller! Bouffy, go and tell them to clear off, would you?"

Bouffard nodded, his heart sinking, but his father had already wandered out of the room.

He reappeared quickly. "Dashed strange, Jorja, there's a blank frag at the door says we owe it a night's lodging."

The Queen blinked. "I've never heard anything so ridiculous!"

"Well, that's what I said, but it seemed pretty sure of itself. Something about a multiscan? I said we didn't want any."

From the palace doors, they then heard a clear voice, singing:

Open the door, my fleet-footed prince

Open the door though it may makes you wince.

And mind the words that we both had to did speak

Out there on the rocks, where the steam shafts leak.

In the pause that followed, Prince Bouffard became aware that both his parents were looking towards him in a fairly pointed fashion.

"Oh, yes. Forgot to mention. The scanner did take a bit of a tumble out by a blowhole due East of here. A passing frag fished it out for me, though, so no harm done."

Spearing a quail's tongue with her fork, the Queen frowned down the table at her only son. "I see. And would this 'passing frag' have any reason to expect bed and board?"

"Ah, I'm afraid I did make a few rash... undertakings," said the Prince, "but I did rather think I'd never see it or the scanner ever again."

"A good practical lesson in politics, then," replied his mother. "You were daft enough to make those promises. Now you have to stick to 'em."

"To a frag? You're joking!"

"Excuse me? I'm bloody not."

Prince Bouffard stood, ready to argue. "You make all sorts of promises you don't -"

The Queen cut him off with a wave, still quite calm. "Yes, and I understand the consequences if I do break 'em, before I open my mouth."

She steepled her royal fingers under her chin for a moment. "No... let it in, keep your promise. A talking frag... Tuesday lost... I want it where we can see it, I need to look into this."

***

The door was opened, and the Frag squelched its way inside. "Good evening, your Majesty," it said to the Queen, "no, don't worry about a chair, bits of me slop over the edge. I'll just sit on the table and nibble from your son's plate if that's all right?"

The three royals exchanged glances, but the King spoke first. "Of course, old chap. We don't tend to, ah, stand on ceremony here."

So Prince Bouffard, fuming under the amused gaze of his parents, heaved the Frag up on to the dining table. It nuzzled up happily to the Prince's plate, and pressed its lumpy pale skin against the Prince's half-eaten samosa, absorbing the minced hummingbird's nutrients by osmosis.

Amused as she was by Prince Bouffard's discomfiture, the Queen watched the undulating mass bouncing around on her dining table with palpable queasiness. As the Prince set down his knife and fork with finality, she took a moment to whisper in the King's ear.

"You'd better ask the housedroids to stand down the dessert. I don't think any of us are going to fancy blancmange tonight."

When the meal was finished (and this did not take long, as no one except the Frag seemed to have much enthusiasm), the King stretched his arms and yawned, grinning at the venomous stare this earned him from his son.

"Well, who's for an early night?"

And so Prince Bouffard was forced to lead the Frag to his room, and to carry it up most of the stairs. The door to the dining room had not quite closed when he heard his parents begin to laugh. "I hope you're enjoying yourself," Bouffard hissed.

"Wouldn't have missed it for the world," replied the Frag.

They finally reached the Prince's room, and he opened the door only with great reluctance. The Frag oozed over the threshold, and sat just in front of the doorway, quivering.

"Such finery," it said, apparently taking in the ornate wooden bed that Bouffard had spent an afternoon making the housedroids carve after the replicator had spat out the flat-pack without any engravings at all.

It was probably the only four poster bed in the Universe with woodcut images of a long-haired man fending off dragon attacks by standing on a mountain and playing a guitar. In spite of himself, Bouffard appreciated the Frag's good taste.

"So are we topping and tailing or what? If not, I

call big spoon!" The Frag called after Bouffard as the Prince stalked into his bathroom to wash the Frag's sharp chemical tang from his hands.

Once the Prince had finished his ablutions, he hoisted the Frag on to the bed as promised, but still stood by in his outdoor clothes and heavy boots.

The Frag squirmed up the duvet to the Prince's own pillow. "No wonder you get up late, this is well comfy!"

"What's going on here?" Bouffard demanded. "You shouldn't be able to speak, and you certainly shouldn't have these ridiculous notions in your head, Frag!"

The Frag did not reply, but instead nuzzled against the little dent the Prince's head had made in the pillow over the years, rubbing against a few strands of hair that had stayed behind that morning.

"My parents might think this is very funny, but you're going out of your way to humiliate me and I must know why!"

The Frag retreated to the middle of the bed. "This isn't a humiliation, Bouffard," it said slowly and deliberately, in a very different voice. "This is a revolution."

With those words, the Frag began to quiver, and then to shake. The Prince stepped back for a moment in alarm, but leaned closer as he saw the Frag begin to stretch. The fine hair began to thicken, to lengthen, and to flow across the Frag's convulsing body.

A crude limb punched its way out of the Frag's body, narrowly missing the Prince's chin. As he recovered from the shock he watched as it formed a clear knee, calf, foot and ankle.

"I had to gain access to you, my prince," the Frag said calmly as it bucked and writhed with its newly found appendages. "I had to assimilate your food in order to empathise with you. I had to experience your habitat in order to remember you. And I had to sample your discarded DNA... in order to become you."

Bouffard had heard enough. He dived forward, ignoring the stabbing pain from his boot, and scooped up the metamorphosing Frag in his arms. With a cry of rage and exertion he flung the twisting thing against the wall of his room.

The Frag hit the wall with a resounding crack, and slid to the ground slowly.

Prince Bouffard sat on his bed, and closed his eyes for a long moment.

When he opened them, a naked man stood before him, with only the tiniest ripples of flesh around the neck betraying the Frag's nature. With a start, the Prince recognised his own golden hair, his own clear blue eyes, and his own athletic form.

"Kinetic energy, great catalyst, thanks," purred the Frag, through lips that were an exact copy of the Prince's own.

"What?"

"We frags aren't the vacant meatsacks you choose to believe we are. We've long been planning for this day, training our natural affinity to mutate genetic code so that one of us could finally gain access to royal DNA before imprinting, and liberate our people. I never thought I would be the one."

The Prince stood up from the bed with a cry, but the Frag sent him crashing to the ground by scything his legs from under him with a single fluid kick.

"Be good, my prince, and I may yet let you live. You are the tool of our salvation, after all. And once I've usurped your place in the palace, why would I need to kill you?"

The Prince gaped. "But how? You're just one man, and my parents will see through your disguise immediately."

The Frag gave a cruel smile, and shook his head. "My prince," he said with heavy sarcasm, "Your genetic template is a fusion of the good King and Queen, and the bioprocessor hidden in my body's every cell can unravel it in a trice."

With that the Frag took up the Prince's knife and, bending straight-legged from the waist, sliced the big toe from both of his own feet. The Prince shuffled away on his backside in horror as thick gouts of blood spurted from the Frag's mutilated feet. The Frag swayed and looked unsteady for a moment, though it might have been as much the adjustment to his balance as the shock or pain of the self-inflicted wound.

Standing at the centre of a puddle of his own blood, the Frag held a severed big toe in each hand, and said simply: "Come."

The Prince whimpered as the door burst open and two blank frags oozed through into the bedchamber. They did not speak, but were soon flanking the impostor Prince, whose blood stained their glowing white bodies, giving them the look of maggots crawling on a wound.

The Frag raised his arms above his head, blood still dripping from the toe in each hand. "My brothers... now will you become my parents."

He flung the toes down on to the undulating backs of the blank frags. The appendages were absorbed straight into the waiting globules, which bucked and writhed at the cuckoo prince's sides.

As the two new frags started thrusting out limbs and new thick hair, Bouffard tried to pull himself to his shaky feet. "It will never work, the housedroids..."

"We have your genetic template to take on your physical forms, and through this palace's records we can piece together your personality and memory imprints. It's already happening, a technology you hardwired into us at the production plant yourselves."

The Frag Queen was beginning to pull herself to her shapeless feet now, a plummy rich voice forcing through her half-formed mouth. "You've sent us to die a billion deaths in senseless battles on airless rocks. Now sit and watch your empires crumble, unless you want to join your multiscan at the bottom of a blowhole."

Prince Bouffard stood up smoothly. Perhaps he had no chance, but he knew he had to act before the two new frags had completed their transformation. They were still vulnerable while they were changing, surely? He raised his fists and, as he looked into his double's eyes, was surprised to see tears in the Frag Prince's eyes.

***

Later, in the middle of the night, the frags dragged the three bodies out to the blowhole. The King and Queen slipped into the depths without a sound, but the new Prince Bouffard was still barefoot from hacking off his big toes, and bent towards his dead template.

"Come away," said the new King, "the memory imprint will begin in minutes. We'll be paralysed for at least twenty-four hours, we must get inside!"

The new Prince had pulled off the corpse's boots, and stared down at the body for a moment. The dead Bouffard had also been missing both big toes.

"A whole day," he said. "We'll miss Tuesday."

With a shrug, he shoved the body into the blowhole, and followed his fellow frags back towards the palace's terraformed grounds.

The rocky ground tormented his own mutilated feet, and he pulled on the boots.

THE DEBT WE ALL MUST PAY

by L F Robertson

It's alright, Princess.

Did I ever tell you why I became a doctor? It was a stupid dream. No, not the idea, I mean it really was... a stupid... dream. I was the youngest son in a large family. There were thirteen of us, all in all. Yes, thirteen, very impressive, no wonder mother died--oh, don't make that face, Princess, it was a long time ago. I never knew her; she died giving birth to me. I suppose thirteen really is an unlucky number. Anyway, this left my father alone with the thirteen of us, and since we were too poor for him to turn to drinking or gambling to forget his problems, he turned to religion instead. My father always was a weak-spirited fool.

Oh, be quiet, Princess, I'll call him whatever I damn well please. He was my father, wasn't he?

Well... one of them, anyway. You see, in a rare, bright moment my father hit on the idea of sharing the burden. He took to the streets of his little rats-piss village to seek the charity of strangers. He was looking for a godfather for his newborn son--me--he told anyone who had the misfortune to cross his path, as for all his 'Hail Mary's and pious flagellation he was still naught but an old sinner, and he was desirous of a firm and caring hand to help raise his infant son in a moral and virtuous manner. Keep me on the straight and narrow, as it were. Frankly, I imagine the old man was always more concerned I be raised in a suitable financial manner than a virtuous one. What? You think that shows caring? It was more for his benefit than mine. Apparently religious fervour doesn't sustain oneself as much as father hoped.

I don't really know what happened, though I suspect most people laughed in his face. The way he used to tell it, people were practically lining up for the honour, but strangely he took issue with all of them. What a load of rot. Although... what? What about the Church? Oh, I see. Yes, I suppose that would have been the most obvious place to go for a handout, but for some reason, from that day on the Church's doors were closed to him. Maybe God offered to be my godfather and he declined, hah!

I always assumed he hadn't found anyone, for there was no sudden appearance of a generous new father figure in my life. Though there was once, just once, when I was ten years old, and my father laid a hand on my shoulder and told me, "You'll be a great man someday, son, a great doctor."

What? Yes, yes, I suppose he was right, now shut-up and listen, Princess.

His warm affection was rare enough that the comment stuck in my mind, and for a time, I assumed that was what caused the dream. After all, I was just a little boy. Don't all little boys look up to their fathers and want to please them?

I was eleven when I had the dream. It was a full year since my father had offered me his sage wisdom. A year to the day.

I dreamed I was in a forest. It seemed as though it should have frightened me, for the trees were hundreds of feet tall, with thick, dark trunks that would have taken ten men to encircle them. The tops of the trees seemed to stretch on for miles, and the thick canopy woven by their leaves should have been claustrophobic, for little light slipped through it, yet I wasn't afraid. I ran from tree to tree, touching each one, and though the ground was wet and slippery, I never lost my footing. After a time, I became aware of someone following me, though it felt more as though my pursuer were keeping an eye on me rather than chasing me.

After a time, I turned. He was just a man, no one I knew. He dressed in plain, dark clothes, the occasional tear or mud splatter suggesting he"d been travelling the woods for some time. Yet despite his dirt-marked appearance, he struck me as a neat individual. His skin was pale, with thin lips set in a narrow line that belied neither approval nor disapproval. His hair was straight and dark, parted to one side, and he had old-fashioned sideburns that followed the cut of his cheekbones. He was no one special, but his eyes… Princess, in those dark, grey eyes was an intensity that you felt sure would catch you and burn you up if you gazed into them too long.

Ah, yes. I thought that would get your attention. Don't worry, Princess. It's all right. I won't let you burn up.

He told me he had something to show me. I told him I wouldn't walk with strangers, and he offered me his hand. "Why," he said, "I'm no stranger. I'm your godfather."

So I took his hand and followed him, deeper and deeper into those dark woods. In time, we came to a clearing. In the middle of the clearing, a single plant grew. My godfather gestured to it with one hand and drew me closer to it. This is for you," he told me. "One day, you will be a doctor. Whenever you are summoned to a sick person, I shall appear on each occasion. If I stand at the head of the patient, you can firmly declare that you'll make him well again. Then, give him some of the herb and he'll recover. However, if I stand at the feet of a patient, he's mine, and you must say there's nothing you can do, and no doctor in the world can save him."

I wanted to ask him questions, say something, but then he let go of my hand, and turned to me, and there was nothing I could say under the full intensity of that gaze. "But beware that you don't use the herb against my will," he told me, and I couldn't imagine that I'd ever dare defy him. "Or you shall be in for trouble."

After that, well, I simply woke up. My godfather's words still rang in my ears, and I felt as though his eyes would be burned into my soul forever, yet still in time I came to dismiss it as nothing but a dream. Why wouldn't I? But then, two years later, on my thirteenth birthday, I received a letter through the post. Inside was a sprig of that very same herb, with an unsigned note beside it written in a cursive script that simply said, "A Christening gift."

I knew then that it had not simply been a dream.

You know, Princess, had I told that story to anyone else they would have laughed at me. Sneered at me. Called me mad. But not you. Are you simply humouring me, I wonder, or simply… but never mind. The rest even you should be able to put together. It all came to pass, as they told me it would. I became a doctor. In time, I became famous. People said that I only need glance at a patient to know the condition and whether they would live or die. I was rich, successful…

So how did we get here, you and I? I, sitting against a wall trying to catch breath that grows shorter every minute, and you, next to me, comforting hand on my shoulder and not a single useful thought in your pretty, empty head?

Oh, shut-up, Princess, and don't make that face, it makes you look ugly, and then you have very little going for you at all. It's not the fever talking, I don't even have a fever, you stupid girl. Urgh. How did we get here indeed… shall I tell you how?

It began with your father. Yes, he was fortunate to have me as his doctor, wasn't he? He should have died, you know. No, I don't mean that as indication of how serious his condition was and how lucky he was, I mean he should have died.

So, your father, Lord Whatever. He was sick, Princess, very sick, but… also very rich. When I went to his bedside I was more concerned with the latter than the former. I spoke to him softly, gently, told him everything would be alright. Then I looked up, and my godfather looked back at me from the foot of the bed. He didn't say anything. He never did.

Normally this would be the point where I'd express my sincerest regrets, and delicately break the news that there was nothing I, nor anyone, could do. Instead, I thought to cheat my godfather--I knew he'd be angry, but I hoped that since I was his godson he'd forgive the trespass. After all, isn't that what family is for? So I took hold of the headboard, and I dragged the bed clockwise so that my godfather stood at your father's head, and then I administered the herb. I could feel his eyes on the back of my neck the whole time, burning.

"Well, you've pulled the wool over my eyes." He intoned from behind me. I did not turn to face him, and I couldn't say whether that was boldness or fear. "I'll forgive you this once because you're my godson. But if you try it again, you'll be risking your own neck. I myself shall come and take you away."

After that, well, I thought all would be well. I was richly rewarded for saving your father's life, and became even more prestigious than before. I didn't think I'd have cause to turn against my godfather's words, but then there was you.

Yes, you. Do you remember our introduction? When I was brought to your sickbed by your despairing father? He was half-grieving already, you know, he was ready to promise me everything if only I could help you. Wealth beyond my wildest dreams, the eternal friendship of a powerful man... his beautiful daughter's hand in marriage.

Yes, yes, of course I think you're beautiful. Even lying in your bed with sickness coursing through your veins and fever ravaging your body you were still beautiful. You managed a smile for me when I came in, and I said... I told you... yes, I know what I said. I told you that you looked like a princess. I do remember.

Your father left the room, and when I finally tore my eyes from your face, I saw my godfather standing at the foot of your bed. No, you're right, Princess, you're not dead, how dreadfully astute. I thought it might all begin to click into place but I see I'll have to tell the tale a little longer. I recalled my godfather's warning, of course. His threat. But I couldn't let you die. Hah, don't look at me like that, girl, it was hardly a choice born of altruism.

So, once more I turned the bed. I gave you the herb. Your condition improved almost immediately; colour returned to your cheeks and you ceased drifting in and out of consciousness. I was just taking your pulse… when I felt a cold hand close on my shoulder, and pull me backwards. I pulled you with me. I'm sorry, Princess, I didn't mean to.

When we awoke we were, well, here. In this charming little cave. Of course, I actually woke sometime before you did… but perhaps you'd already realised that. Shall I tell you what happened in the interim, Princess, what passed in this ungodly place while you slept?

"It's all over for you," My godfather told me. "Now it's your turn to die."

Don't tell me I'm not dying, girl, which one of us is the doctor? It doesn't matter how strongly my heart beats beneath your hand, or how many pretty tears you cry. My metaphorical hourglass is running out of sand. Can you picture that pile of sand, girl? What good are a few drops of water in the desert?

He left, and, well, that brings us to now.

Wait, did you hear that?

Ah, and here, the patient's final visitor. Why do you bring a candle, godfather? Is it a candle to light me to bed? It's… so dark. Your candle is almost out.

He's right there, girl, are you blind? Can't you see him?

The candle is… it's my candle. It's almost out. Please, please keep it burning, godfather. Please, it's so dark.

I'm not babbling, rot you.

Please, godfather. Please. Light another candle. Don't let it go out. Please.

No!

It's alright, Princess. It's alright, it's alright, it's al—

FAIRY OBVIOUS: AN ESSAY

by Julius Horne

"It was a dark and stormy night. Six brigands sat around the campfire. Their leader said 'Eli, tell us a story', and this is the story Eli told:

'It was a dark and stormy night. Six brigands sat around the campfire. Eli said "Jack, tell us a story", and this is the story Jack told:

"It was a dark and stormy night. Six brigands sat around the campfire. Jack said "Thomas, tell us a story", and this is the story Thomas told:

'It was a dark and stormy night. Six brigands sat around the campfire. Thomas turned to the leader and said "Tell us a story".

"'It's time for bed," the leader said. So they all returned to their tents and went to sleep'"'''".

No doubt you have heard it before. Sometimes it is a Captain and his shipmates. Sometimes there is a gale blowing or the rain falls in torrents. The opening line goes back as far as Edward Bulwer-Lytton's 1830 novel, Paul Clifford, but it has been used many times since, and none can say for sure from whence it came, although we can see its purpose—to tell a story within a story to avoid telling a story. But what is it? Do you know your fairy stories from your fables? Your shaggy dogs from your weird fiction? Your myths from your legends? Or perhaps you think they may be one and the same. Whatever you may think, don't let the academics dictate what you believe, get your hands dirty and, like me, read, collect, compare and read again.

Nowadays a collector of folk tales is lauded as an anthropologist, a scientist concerned with the history of the medium and the evolution of cultural beliefs. But it wasn't always so. Aesop may have given us the first fables, and if we set Greek myth aside, it is Tacitus who was the first recorded collector of anecdotes, if not stories, struggling to distinguish between fact and fiction. But it was not until the nineteenth century, following the publication of Grimm's *Household Tales* (Jakob and Wilhelm Grimm – 1812, 1815) that we saw the eminence of the fairy tale, no doubt facilitated by the ease of travel through Europe and beyond. Where the Grimms sought to capture local culture for posterity, eager Imperialists were keen to collect, translate and claim not just historic artefacts, but also the flavour of foreign cultures. Without what we now think of as vandalism and appropriation, it has been the work of these folklorists that preserved tales endangered by the growth of cities and the rise of published literature. It is a long list that includes Samuel Laing (Snorri Sturlson's *Heimskringla* – 1844), Sir Richard Burton (*A Thousand and One Nights* – 1850), Joel Chandler Harris (*Uncle Remus, His Songs and His Sayings; The Folk-Lore of the Old Plantation* – 1881), W R S Ralston (*The Songs of the Russian People* – 1882), Helen Zimmern (*Ferdowski's Shah Namah of Persia* – 1883), George Dasent (*Popular Tales from the Norse* – 1904), Lewis Spence (*Hero Tales and Legends of the Rhine* – 1915) and Arthur Ransome (*Old Peter's Russian Tales* – 1916).

Tales once told around the fire, by word of mouth, were prized as the closes thing to a primary source these curious men – travellers far and wide in search of new stories – were seeking. Each iteration, however slight the change, was captured and recorded so that the story's journey could be pieced together from the subtle clues and shifts in narrative. There was no differentiation – folk stories were folk stories, they needed neither rhyme nor reason, nor did they need to be tales of consequence.

These tales influenced the content and structure of the first original works associated with the field. Hans Christian Andersen's *Eventyr*, published between 1840 and 1845, along with the later works of the Scottish author George MacDonald, established the fairy tale as the most popular form of children's tale. Original, symbolic, and resonant with what had gone before, it was this body of work that influenced the works of Lewis Carroll, E Nesbit, Enid Blyton, JRR Tolkien, C S Lewis and even G K Chesterton.

Of course, all good things come to an end, and in 1910 the first Folk Tale classification system (the Aarne-Thompson Motif Index) was introduced, and folkloristics was born. It does a good job of cataloguing plots, grouping themes and providing a basis for comparative analysis, but it contributed towards a rift between anthropology and literary criticism, and the folk tale came to be defined by its structures, its component parts, the roles within it and the functions that the narrative serves. In recent years this seems to have changed, with alternative perspectives offered by other disciplines such as anthropology (Campbell's comparative mythology, for example), psychology (Jungian Archetypes and their successors), sociology (social history in particular) and linguistics. Yet still the classification goes on, and the tales we tell—be they tall or cautionary tales passed down through our family and culture or the half remembered anecdotes picked up in everyday life—must fight to be recognised for what they are. Perhaps the most powerful statement on the matter comes from Joseph Campbell, who said that "wherever the poetry of myth is interpreted as biography, history, or science, it is killed" (*The Hero With a Thousand Faces* – 1949).

But, thanks to folkloristics, we have some differentiation:

A *fable* is an explicitly moral fiction that uses animals and other beasts as a proxy for humans to illustrate action and consequence, and to use maxims to emphasise right and wrong, or common sense and foolhardiness.

A *fairy tale* is a short folkloric fantasy that features nonsensical or unbelievable elements such as fantasy kingdoms, magical beasts and enchanted locales. It usually (more by custom than practice) has a happy ending.

A *legend* is a folk narrative passed down and most commonly presented as historic truth or, at the very least, as rooted in such truth.

A *myth* is a narrative held sacred by the culture from which it comes. This is usually differentiated from legend by being pre-historic in origin, telling stories relating to the origins of the culture.

A *tall tale* is on too heavily exaggerated to be believed, but offered for the purposes of good humoured entertainment.

A *shaggy dog story* is an often long-winded and

pointless tale whose anticlimactic humour is based upon keeping the listener's attention to the very end, evoking a groan rather than a laugh.

But regardless of how they are defined, these are all folk tales, having passed, both orally and by written record, through the cultural sphere to be used and repeated at will. They are owned by everyone, copyrighted to nobody, and are well enough known that they can be recited at a moment's notice—just like every fireside tale. Speaking of which, the story told at the head of this essay is a shaggy dog story that I first heard from my grandmother at the age of three or four. She would stretch it out until all six men had said their piece, and she gave each of them funny voices, but I was usually asleep by then. And that's what fairy tales are for. Bedtime stories for children, young and old.

EDITOR'S AFTERWORD

by Colin Fisher

As the latest volume of rewritten fairy tales from Fringeworks finally sees the light of day, we have to commend those of you who have had the patience (and discernment) to bear with us through the stormy waters that lie between commissioning and publication. That this volume has tacked a slightly more tortuous course against the headwind is testament to our desire that Vol 4 represent a strengthening of our ongoing commitment to quality across the board.

Whilst it would have been easy to follow in the wake of the previously published volumes, we felt that this latest in the series provided an opportunity to raise the bar, both in terms of design and story selection. Furthermore, since it is undeniable that 'fairy tale' inspired fiction has become over the last few years a somewhat crowded market, publishers need to adopt fresh approaches to persuade readers perhaps overwhelmed with choice to part with hard earned cash. All of which brings its own challenges. By their very nature Fairy Tales can seem overly traditional and familiar, and we whilst we know that for many this is the undoubted attraction (and has led to the modern resurgence in popularity), just as many look for new interpretations and imaginings, for old friends in unexpected guises and places. In a crowded market place sometimes the quietly different stand out the most.

We would also like to thank our contributors for patience above and beyond the call of duty. Unfortunately for those selected for these later volumes, all stories up to and including the forthcoming volume 5 were contracted from an initial submission call, which has meant waiting in a queue which sometimes seemed like it might never move forward for each successive volume to appear. Finally, your turn has come, and we hope this latest volume has not only proven worth the wait for contributors and readers alike, but has gone some way toward satisfying – if only temporarily – the appetite for all things fairy tale, whether ancient, modern or futuristic.

CONTRIBUTOR BIOGRAPHIES

COLIN FISHER - EDITOR

Colin is a sometime writer and longtime idler living among the detritus of London's unfashionable outskirts. He has published several perfunctory and wholly risible stories among the lower class of independent publisher, together with equally lack-of-noteworthy poetry in the sort of narcissistic and ephemeral presses that define the word 'small.' In a previous existence, he produced and edited a low grade sf and fantasy newsletter for a national bookshop chain, which was avidly read by no-one of any consequence. He has one interminable unfinished novel and an abandoned thesis on Roman charcoal to his name, and hopes to not finish another novel sometime in 2016.

He is the author of 'Speakingland', an unperformable libretto, while his irredeemably flawed short fiction includes such titles as 'Daniel Silence, *Gentleman*', 'The Emissary Goat' and 'Snow White, Throat White'. His latest attempt at a meaningful narrative, a pretentious and derivative novella called 'The Incorruptible Sinner,' was completed in 2015. True to form, this remains unpublished.

Co-opted by Fringeworks as part of a moribund charity project, Colin now finds himself applying his usual pococurantism to the unsuspecting contributors of Grimm and Grimmer, vols 3-5. He has no sense of humour, and earns pennies from sneering pedestrians by dancing with a supercilious cat.

COVER ARTIST - PAPER PANDA

Paper Panda started in 2010, with Louise Firchau making typographical lyrical papercuts from recycled paper. Since then PP has grown significantly and now has a number of very distinct styles and a multitude of merchandise so that everyone can have a piece of the original bear.

The 'Woodland Friends' series of papercuts have been hand drawn and hand cut by Louise. They are inspired by Quarwood, where the Panda family lived in a little cottage in the Cotswolds surrounded by animals and woodland life.

The Storybook series (and other gothic darkness) is a cute collaboration between Mr & Mrs Panda. Louise tells Ryan what to draw with a waggy, pointy finger over his shoulder and only when he gets it perfectly right she cuts it out of paper. It's a good bit of teamwork.

The typographical pieces are created using digital software. Louise studied typography at university and it became an obsession. "There is nothing more satisfying than creating a piece of graphic art using amazing fonts and hand cutting it so perfectly that no matter what the size it looks like it's been printed."

Now Paper Panda has it's own extensive range of giftware that can be found in the online shop including an amazing 'Guest Artist' section, as well as it's own Papercutting and Swapping/Selling Facebook groups.

Everything that has been created is either made in house, or by small UK businesses wherever possible. Louise has taught thousands of people to papercut through online groups using our papercutting starter kit (also available in the shop).

Website: www.paperpandacuts.co.uk

Facebook: www.facebook.com/PaperPandaPapercuts

Etsy: www.etsy.com/uk/shop/PaperPandaPapercuts

AUTHORS

Sara Taylor grew up in Virginia, ran away to England for an education, and disappoints her parents by showing no inclination to return to the States. In between thesis meetings she mostly gets lost, gets rained on, and gets chased by cows. Her first novel, The Shore, is being published by Random House in 2015, and contains an improbable amount of sex, violence, and wild ponies. Her short fiction can be found in print and online.

David Thomas Moore is the third and youngest son of an ogre and a princess. He was smuggled out to Australia to prevent his monstrous father from eating him, and raised by humble clerical workers. He lives in Reading, Berkshire, with his wife Tamsin and daughter Beatrix – herself a changeling child deposited by the goblins – where he awaits a visit by three talking animals (or possibly dwarves), who will give him knowledge and magic to complete his quest. David is the commissioning editor for Abaddon Books, until such time as he receives the call to arms to outwit the ogre, free his mother and take the throne of his father's magical kingdom. If you learn and speak his true name, he will grant you one wish.

Julius Horne (1906-2006) was a Staffordshire storyteller whose works went unpublished during his lifetime. A raconteur, a practising white magician, a collector of folk tales and other arcane stories, he claimed that many of his tales were drawn from real life, and that truth will always be stranger than fiction.

Kirstin Fulton is an academic turned creative writer who makes a living in corporate content development. She is the founder of Ink and Arc Editing and Story Design, a service for flourishing writers in need of creative support. She has published several short works in The Boulevard, a publication of the Attic Institute, and is working on her first novel. Kirstin has her M.A. in French from UCLA, which she intends to make some good use of through fusion of fantasy and French literary themes in her work. She lives in Portland, OR.

Leland Thoburn is the name commonly given to an ancient, lowly scribe whose works are occasionally found in shattered urns sprinkled throughout Mesopotamia. Archeologists believe that he lived a

Spartan existence, huddled in fear and loathing as far away from then-popular culture as possible. Amazingly, forty-nine of this literary Luddite's works have been accepted for publication. Many can be found at Leland Thoburn, Storyteller, a web site maintained by a cult of his followers.

Andrew Lawston lives in London with a small black cat, where he spends his evenings writing strange stories, acting in local theatre productions for charity, and planning a Dordogne wedding with his fiancée Melanie. He enjoys cooking and eating Indian food, and is a lifelong Doctor Who fan. Andrew was first published in the 2000 Doctor Who charity anthology The Cat That Walked Through Time. After a brief teaching career, he moved on to original fiction with Throwing Up With the Joneses, published in e-zine Leafing Through in 2005. Too Much Love Can Kill You and The Hero Function followed in long defunct publications in 2006 and 2007, before Andrew returned to Doctor Who fan fiction, contributing Pierrot le Who? to Shelf Life, the anthology produced as a tribute to the late Craig Hinton. After a few years devoted to writing non-fiction articles under a pseudonym, Andrew self-published a collection of his original fiction in 2012, under the title Something Nice – 10 Stories. In November 2013, he followed this, as one does, by self-publishing his MPhil thesis on the depiction of violence in the early films of Jean-Luc Godard.In 2014, he self-published his translation of Giacomo Casanova's autobiographical novel Histoire de Ma Fuite (Story of My Escape). Andrew continues to submit short stories to anthologies, as well as working on a further self-published story collection, and on a novel project.

L F Robertson lives in some part of England that, if pressed, she would broadly define as London. This ambiguity is largely down to the fact that Lucy has noticed new friends are much less likely to try and drop in if they can only narrow your address down to within 600 miles. She seems to derive some enjoyment from writing about human suffering and misery, which is also incidentally her one glowing qualification as an employee in Human Resources. There she can be found disillusioning the optimistic peons who, despite significant evidence to the contrary, seem to be under the impression she's there to help them, and is often observed slithering away from more persistent characters after stunning them with a barrage of lies, false promises and misinformation.

Old wives whisper that, when the moon is full, she emerges from her lair of misplaced paperwork and old shopping bags to leave disjointed ravings masquerading as short stories on the desk of anyone who looks distracted enough to simply sweep them up with more worthy submissions. These pieces of paper may or may not bear a runic inscription that will draw a powerful demon to you unless passed on with due haste to some other unsuspecting sap. She denies insinuating publishing said pieces of paper would amount to much the same thing.

STORIES

The stories in Grimm & Grimmer volume 4 are based, in order, upon the following fairy tales:

The Robber Bridegroom
Bearskin
Three Billy Goats Gruff / Chitty Chitty Bang Bang / The Hobbit / The Pied Piper of Hamelin
The Mouse, the Bird and the Sausage
Cinderella / Snow White
The Frog Prince
Godfather Death

FIND OUT MORE ABOUT
FRINGEWORKS BY SCANNING
THE QR CODE BELOW

WWW.FRINGEWORKS.CO.UK

www.ingramcontent.com/pod-product-compliance
Lightning Source LLC
Chambersburg PA
CBHW070628130626
46555CB00006B/2475